實用
中英翻譯法

彭登龍 著

五南圖書出版公司 印行

序

　　誠如本書的標題所示，本書《實用中英翻譯法》對理論很少著墨，而是把重點放在中英翻譯方法的實例解析與應用，期盼能協助讀者立即應用於中英翻譯或口譯領域。

　　中英文翻譯一般都有基本方法或技巧可資遵循，包括中英翻譯的三個基本方法與轉換法六個技巧。中英翻譯的三個基本方法為：（1）增加法（Adding Approach）；（2）減少法（Subtracting Approach）；（3）轉換法（Transforming Approach）。然後，詳細介紹中英翻譯轉換法中的六種技巧，包括：（1）改變技巧（Changing Skill）；（2）拆句技巧（Splitting Skill）；（3）合併技巧（Combining Skill）；（4）肯定句／否定句交換技巧（Affirmative/Negative Switching Skill）；（5）重組技巧（Restructuring Skill）；（6）綜合技巧（Synthesizing Skill）。作者將其思想轉化為原文（source language）文字或語言，而譯者則需運用翻譯的基本方法或技巧來探索並解讀作者的原意，然後翻譯成為譯文（translated language）的文字或語言。

　　編者在大學任教中英翻譯課時，深感學生因為不熟悉上述的基本方法與技巧，以致於在面對英文原文書、英文文章或研究論文時，常因無法快速地掌握翻譯要領而倍感挫折與壓力。學生若能運用中英文翻譯方法與技巧，應有助其提升翻譯品質與效率。因此，編者彙集任教於大學中英翻譯課程的上課內容、教學經驗和心得成書，分享快速掌握中英文翻譯的訣竅，期望有助於讀者打造高效的中英文翻譯力。

　　編者希望本書能為讀者精進中英文翻譯方法與技巧貢獻綿薄之力。唯編者才疏學淺，復因付梓匆促，書中難免有所疏漏，尚祈各位先進與讀者不吝賜教。

彭登龍 敬上

本書內容簡介

　　本書共分為三章。**第一章**為中英翻譯概論，包含前言、翻譯的定義、中英文的差異、中英翻譯的三大標準、中英文的文化思考模式、找英文主詞與動詞的方法。**第二章**介紹中英翻譯的三個基本方法與轉換法六個技巧，即三個基本方法：（1）增加法（Adding Approach）；（2）減少法（Subtracting Approach）；與（3）轉換法（Transforming Approach）。接著詳細介紹中英翻譯轉換法六種技巧，包括：（1）改變技巧（Changing Skill）——字、詞類、語態、句型；（2）拆句技巧（Splitting Skill）；（3）合併技巧（Combining Skill）；（4）肯定句否定句交換技巧（Affirmative/Negative Switching Skill）；（5）重組技巧（Restructuring Skill）；（6）綜合技巧（Synthesizing Skill）。**第三章**為綜合練習，包含英文長句的斷句與翻譯練習、中英文句子翻譯的練習、中英文段落翻譯的練習、中英文文章翻譯的練習、相關考試歷屆試題解析（包含各類公職中英翻譯試題練習與解析、教育部中英文翻譯能力檢定考試試題練習與解析）。

　　有關中英翻譯的三個基本方法與轉換法六個技巧，請看下一頁圖表。

翻譯方法與技巧簡表：

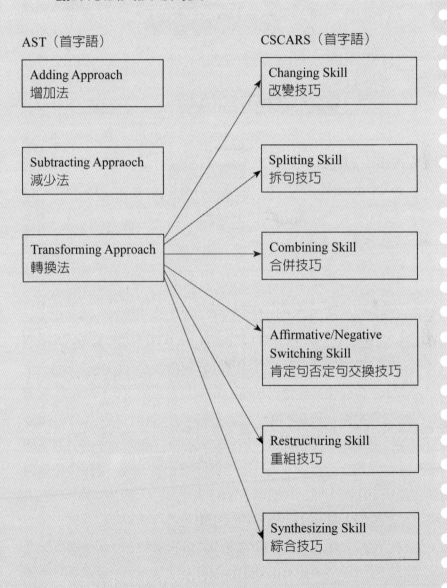

AST（首字語）

CSCARS（首字語）

Adding Approach
增加法

Subtracting Appraoch
減少法

Transforming Approach
轉換法

Changing Skill
改變技巧

Splitting Skill
拆句技巧

Combining Skill
合併技巧

Affirmative/Negative
Switching Skill
肯定句否定句交換技巧

Restructuring Skill
重組技巧

Synthesizing Skill
綜合技巧

目錄

第一章　中英翻譯概論

1-1 前 言（Preface）

　　中英翻譯是大學與研究所學程中的重要課題，而如何有效率地做好中英文翻譯工作、翻譯出詞能達意而道地的中英文，實為當務之急。因此，唯有熟稔中英文翻譯方法與技巧，才能以事半功倍之效，游刃有餘地悠遊於學海之中。

　　編者認為，在熟稔中英文翻譯方法與技巧之前，先需要了解中英文的基本差異與翻譯的三大標準「信、達、雅」。英文翻譯成中文時，以通順暢達為原則；而中文翻譯成英文時，除了明白順暢的原則以外，還需合乎英文語法與句法。總之，不論是英翻中或是中翻英時，譯文必須掌握原文的涵義，符合譯文的文化思考模式、語言習慣用法、語言表達方式（Tan, 2001），而能夠達到嚴復所提倡的「信、達、雅」或思果所主張的「信、達、貼」的要求與標準（吳潛誠，1989；梅德明，2010）。

　　無論是英文本科系或非英文本科系的學生想必大都有如下經驗：大學生時常需要閱讀英文原文書籍或文章，有時候即使透過網路翻譯軟體，所翻譯出來的中文讀起來自己也不明瞭。而國際期刊有80%、網路資訊高達85%均以英文呈現，因此如何在資訊與知識經濟的時代，藉由高效率的閱讀與翻譯第一手的英文資訊以取得新知，便成為渴求提升競爭力之現代知識經濟人的重要課題。有鑑於此，編者彙集任教於大學中英文翻譯課時的上課內容、教學經驗和心得，期望能幫助讀者們在閱讀英文時能快速的掌握重點，以提升英文閱讀與翻譯效率。

1-2 翻譯的定義（Definition of Translation）

多位翻譯方面的名家、學者與研究學人對翻譯有不同的定義與主張，編者茲舉幾位具有代表性的翻譯名家的定義與主張為例，提供讀者參考。

Catford（1965）對翻譯的定義如下："the replacement of textual material in one language (source language) by equivalent textual material in another language (target language)."（p. 20）。翻譯成中文就是：翻譯就是以另一種語言（目標語）中同意義的文本的資料取代一種語言（原文）的文本資料。而關鍵字就是相等的、相同的、同意義的概念。

Wikipedia 對翻譯的定義如下："Translation is the communication of the meaning of a source-language text by means of an equivalent target-language text."翻譯成中文就是：翻譯就是藉由同意義的目標語（譯文）文字，針對原文文字意義的溝通。與Catford（1965）對翻譯的定義為相同的理致，Wikipedia 對翻譯定義的重點也是相等的、相同的、同意義的概念。

林語堂（1967）在〈論翻譯〉一文中指出，翻譯是一種藝術（translation as a fine art），而翻譯藝術所需具備的條件包括：（1）譯者對於原文文字及內容的透徹了解；（2）具有相當國文程度來書寫通順暢達的中文；（3）譯事上的訓練。

思果（2003）在《翻譯研究》一書中提到，「翻譯是藝術，要動手去做的，要想精熟，只有多讀中英文書、多思想、多翻譯。」（p. 13）。他認為把英文譯成中文的基本條件包括：（1）能用中文寫作；（2）懂得英文；（3）有點治學訓練；（4）對文字的敏感；（5）想像力；（6）勤勞精細。

實用中英翻譯法

編者認爲，中英文翻譯以「信、達、雅」爲原則，英文翻譯成中文時，以通順暢達爲原則；而中文翻譯成英文時，以合乎英文語法與句法爲原則。總之，不論是英翻中或是中翻英，譯文必須掌握原文的涵義，符合譯文的文化思考模式（cultural thought patterns）、句法正確道地（syntactic correctness and authenticity）、慣用語法（common expressions）來翻譯，而關鍵在於「熟能生巧」。

 1-3 中英文的差異（Differences between Chinese and English）

　　眾所周知，中英文：（1）字眼不同、句法不同、聲音不同；（2）一個完整的英文句子必須有主詞與動詞；（3）英文主詞與動詞數目的一致性；（4）主詞若是第三人稱單數，現在式的動詞字尾須加上s/es；（5）英文動詞的十二個時態有些複雜；（6）英文的連接詞功能非常重要（思果，2013）。除此之外，下列的差異，對譯者而言，更值得注意。

（一）語言學結構上的差異

- 中文：意合的語言
- 英文：形合的語言

　　由於中西民族文化與心理思維習慣的差異，會反映在語言與寫作上面。一般而言，中文重視悟性、整體抽象、綜合、直覺與意象的概念，而英文重視形式論證、個體思維、分析、理性與邏輯的特點（王斌華、伍志偉，2014）。

　　Nida（1984）指出：中文與英文在語言學結構上最大也是最重要的一個差異，就是意合（parataxis）與形合（hypotaxis）的對比。所謂意合（parataxis），就是指語言組織主要靠句子內部的邏輯關係，注重意義上的連貫（coherence）。所謂形合（hypotaxis），就是指語言組織主要靠語言本身的句法手段，注重語言形式上的接應（cohesion）。大部分的語言學家都同意：中文比較屬於意合的語言，各個詞類像竹子一樣，各自獨立；而英文比較屬於形合的語言，需要連接詞，像樹木一樣。

- Parataxis：意合

【語】並列（一系列相關的子句或片語之間沒有連接詞）（例如："I came, I saw, I conquered."）

Parataxis是從希臘字"parataxis"（para + taxis = beside arrangement）來的，就是指沒有使用連接詞（connectives），句子內部連接或句子間的連接是靠語意的貫通。

中文重意合，指句子內部連接或句子間連接採用語意手段（semantic connection）。中文少用連接詞而用語意來貫通。所以，一般來說，中文句子通常比英文句子短。

- Hypotaxis：形合

【文】從屬

Hypotaxis是從希臘字"hupotaxis"（hupo + taxis = under arrangement）來的，就是指使用連接詞（connectives）來連接對等（coordinate）、附屬（subordinate）、嵌入（embedding）子句或句子內部或連接句子與句子。

英文重形合，指句子內部連接或句子間的連接採用句法手段（syntactic devices）或詞法手段（lexical equivalence）。詞法手段類似語篇學（discourse）裡的銜接手段（cohesion）。如：指代、詞語的重複和照應、省略，還有句子之間的連接詞（包括讓步、轉折、因果等）。所以，一般來說，英文遇到複雜句時則較長。

- Coherence：

指連貫性。Coherence指的是文章整體是否通順，作者的立場前後是否一致，包含文章所採取的立場、段落的中心思想是否一致。

- Halliday（1976）：

Cohesion指接應或聯繫，其所運用的工具（cohesive ties）主要為：指涉（reference）、替代（substitution）、連接（conjunction）、省略（ellipsis）、詞彙聯繫（lexical cohesion）。

思果（2013）在《翻譯新究》一書中強調，譯者最須注意的是一個英文句子裡各單位的連接。針對中英文的分別，他使用的比喻很妙。他將英文句子的結構比喻成九連環或一串珠鍊，英文連在一起一看就看出來。而中文句子卻像一盤珠子，各不銜接，大珠小珠各粒可以單獨放開，串起來或不串起來都可以，不串起來更自然，因為大家心裡都明白，各粒珠子還是串連的，只是不用「環」連接，沒有使用連接詞「是」、「和」，也沒有把修飾語置於名詞前面而已。

茲以元代散曲大家馬致遠的《天淨沙‧秋思》為例，說明中文意合與英文形合語言學結構上的差異。

枯藤老樹昏鴉，小橋流水人家，古道西風瘦馬。
夕陽西下，斷腸人在天涯。

【譯文】
枯藤纏繞著老樹，樹枝上棲息著黃昏時歸巢的烏鴉，小橋下，流水潺潺，旁邊有幾戶人家，在古老荒涼的道路上，秋風蕭瑟，一匹疲憊的瘦馬馱著我蹣跚前行。夕陽向西緩緩落下，悲傷斷腸的人還漂泊在天涯。

【譯文】意合版
Autumn Thoughts: To the Tune of Tian Jin Sha

Withered vine, old tree, crows at dusk,

Tiny bridge, flowing brook, and cottages,

Ancient road, bleak wink, bony steed.

The sun sinking west,

A heart-torn traveler at the end of the world.

(*XCN, Chinese*)

【譯文】形合版

Tian Jing Sha, Autumn Thought

Withered vines are hanging on old branches;

Returning crows are croaking at dusk.

A few houses are hidden past a narrow bridge,

And below the bridge a quiet creek is running.

Down a worn path, in the west wind,

A lean horse comes plodding.

The sun dips down in the west,

And the lovesick traveler is still at the end of the world.

（Adapted from 丁祖馨、Burtton Raffel）

（二）句子結構上的差異

1. 顯著的差異

- 中文：主題顯著（theme prominence）
- 英文：主語（詞）顯著（subject prominence）

中文是主題顯著（theme prominence）的語言，中文句子常常可以省略主語或主詞，所以中文經常使用無主語的句子；而英文是主語或主詞顯著（subject prominence）的語言，所以英文一個完整的句子，除了祈使句以外，必須有主語或主詞。因為中英文有此句子結構上的差異，因此中文翻譯成英文時，必須先找到或確定主語或主詞。

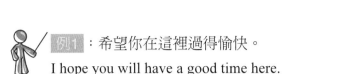

例1：希望你在這裡過得愉快。

I hope you will have a good time here.

I hope you will enjoy yourself here.

I hope you will have fun here.

【解析】：中文句子實際上省略了「我」，因此翻譯成英文時需要增譯「I」。

例2：科學的奧妙與魔術的奇幻曾同時吸引著劉謙，但因為特別喜愛「表演」，所以走上了職業魔術師的路。

Both the wonder of science and the fantasy of magic attracted Lu Chen [Liou Chien] simultaneously. But since he was particularly fond of "performance", Lu decided to embark on the career as a professional magician.

【解析】：中文原文中一個長句裡的數個短句中的主詞可以不相同，而且各短句不需要用連接詞連接，甚至主詞也可以省略，因為中文是一個主題顯著的語言。但是英文是一個主語（詞）顯著的語言，所以各個短句中的主詞必須彰顯，而各短句需要有連接詞做連接。如同英文譯文中第一句的主詞是the wonder of science and the fantasy of magic，第二句的主詞是Lu，這兩個英文句子因為主詞不同，在這裡就需要以句點分開。

第一句中文也可以翻譯成被動語態的英文句子：

Lu Chen [Liou Chien] was fascinated by both the wonder of science and the fantasy of magic simultaneously.

But since he was particularly fond of "performance", he made up his mind to pursue the career as a professional magician.

2. 謂語（predicate）的差異
- 中文：多種詞類可當謂語
- 英文：以動詞為中心的謂語結構

中文裡，除了動詞以外，名詞、形容詞也可以當作謂語。而英文中，動詞才可以當作謂語，英文典型的句子結構是「主語 + 動詞」（subject + verb）。

predicate [ˋprɛdɪkɪt]【語】述語，述部

 例1：度假是發現世界新奇事物的大好機會。

Vacations are great opportunities to discover new things in the world.

【解析】：謂語是名詞「大好的機會」。

例2：我們昨天下榻的旅館很豪華。

The hotel we stayed at yesterday is gorgeous.

【解析】：謂語是形容詞「豪華的」。

3. 修飾詞位置的差異

- 中文：前位修飾
- 英文：後位修飾

中文的結構是：修飾語 + 主要名詞。

英文的結構是：主要名詞 + 修飾語。

英文的後位修飾結構可以下列圖表呈現：

The		Prep. Phrase (of the...)
A + (Adj.) + N. (S.) +	Adj. Clause (who/which + S. V.) + V. (+ O./C.)	
An		P.P. (-ed)
		V+ing

例1：李先生是 我們化學系 畢業的 優秀的 博士生。

【解析】：修飾語：我們化學系

畢業的

優秀的

主要名詞：博士生

Mr. Lee is an outstanding Ph.D. student who graduated from our chemistry department.

【解析】：主要名詞：Ph.D. student

修飾語：an outstanding

who graduated

from our chemistry department

博士生：Ph.D. student, doctoral student

 例2：The rise in global temperature would produce new patterns and extremes of drought and rainfall, seriously disrupting food production in certain regions. (Longman iBT TOEFL: Reading)

【解析】：全球的溫度（修飾語）+ 上升（主要名詞）

 例3：All students who want to use the library borrowing services and the recreational, atheltic, and entertainment facilities must have a valid summer identification card.

【解析】：想要使用圖書館借閱服務與休閒、運動與娛樂設施的（修飾語）+ 所有的學生們（主要名詞）

 例4：Cancers which develop in the lymph nodes and blood are particularly dangerous since these are then spread throughout the rest of the body through the lymphatic system and circulatory system.

(Longman iBT TOEFL: Reading)

【解析】：淋巴結與血液中所發展的（修飾語）+ 癌症（主要名詞）

 例5：Extra greenhouse gases produced by man could cause a serious imbalance and push the Earth faster into a climactic disaster.

(Longman iBT TOEFL: Reading)

【解析】：人所製造的（修飾語）＋額外的溫室氣體（主要名詞）

例6：Brian is a brilliant doctoral student graduating from a prestigious university.

【解析】：畢業於很有名望大學的（修飾語）＋博士生（主要名詞）

 1-4 中英翻譯的三大標準：信、達、雅
（Three Major Criteria in Chinese and English Translation: Faithfulness, Expressiveness, and Elegance）

翻譯的三大標準，大家都耳熟能詳，就是嚴復提倡的「信、達、雅」，不管是英翻中、中翻英，都需要達到「信、達、雅」的要求與標準。而思果主張「信、達、貼」的原則（思果，2003，2014）。

嚴復提倡的信、達、雅：
- 信（**Faithfulness**）：可以忠實地傳達原文的意思，這就是「信」。
- 達（**Expressiveness**）：可以充分地傳達原文的涵義，這就是「達」。
- 雅（**Elegance**）：可以優雅地傳達原文的意境，這就是「雅」。

思果（2003，2014）主張的信、達、貼：
- 信：譯者對原作者負責，把原作者的原意用中文表現出，不要表錯，這就是「信」。
- 達：譯者替讀者服務，雖然作者的原意已經表達出來了，也要讀者能看得懂，才算盡職，這就是「達」。
- 貼：譯文確實，讀者也懂，但是原文的文體、氣勢、身分各方面是否達到恰如其分的地步，這就牽涉是否貼切的問題，也就是「貼」。（pp. 17-18）

編者認為，中英文翻譯以「信、達、雅」為標準，除了嚴復所提倡的「信、達、雅」與思果所主張的「信、達、貼」的翻譯標準以外，英文翻譯成中文時，以通順暢達為原則；而中文翻譯成英文時，以合乎英文語法和句法為原則。總之，不論是英翻中或是中翻英，譯文（translated language）必須掌握原文（source language）的涵義，符合譯文的文化思考模式、句法正確道地、慣用語法來翻譯。

- 文化思考模式（cultural thought patterns）
- 句法正確道地（syntactical correctness and authenticity）
- 慣用語法（common expressions）

　　首先英翻中方面，舉一個很典型的例子，就是《春風化雨》這部電影，原來的英文片名是 "Dead Poets Society"，中國翻譯的片名是《死亡詩社》，這真的是直譯（literal translation, word for word translation）、直接的翻譯、逐字的翻譯，的確有達到「信」的要求與標準，但是尚未達到「達」與「雅」、「貼」。

　　這部電影是由喜劇明星羅賓威廉斯（Robin Williams）所主演，在《春風化雨》電影中飾演一位挑戰保守體制的英文老師。這部戲的背景是在一所專門培育國家棟梁的寄宿學校，這位英文老師帶領這群高中生在保守、傳統的私校中，鼓勵他們不盲從，挑戰保守體制，發揮創意思考。其中一段最令觀眾回味的橋段是，他要學生們將英文課本中，衡量詩句價值的測量表給整頁撕下。還有另一橋段也很發人深省，那就是，為了展示學生與生俱來的特性，他將學生們引領至操場中，告知每個人都有獨一無二的行走方式，鼓勵學生們獨立思考，找回自我。

　　此片的主題，就是這位英文老師，分享其自身經驗，鼓勵這些學生們追求理想，樂觀勇敢面對人生。因此「春風化雨」的翻譯呢？編者認為就是很好的意譯（free translation），充分展現「信」、「達」、「雅」、「貼」的意境。相信看過這部電影的人，都會有此同感！

- Dead Poets Society：《死亡詩社》「信」
- Dead Poets Society：《春風化雨》「信」、「達」、「雅」、「貼」

　　再來舉一個中翻英的例子，「我要給他一點顏色瞧瞧！」若英文翻譯成 "I'll give him some colors to see." 豈不貽笑大方。此句中文可以翻成 "I'll teach him a lesson." "I'll show him what I can do." "I'll let him know what I am capable of." 然而若翻譯成 "I'll show him who the boss is." 則能達到「信」、「達」、「雅」、「貼」的意境。

- I'll teach him a lesson.
- I'll show him what I can do.
- I'll let him know what I am capable of.
- I'll show him who the boss is.

　　最後舉另一個中翻英的例子，「船到橋頭自然直」這句中文諺語所代表的意思就是一切順其自然，最終都會有一個結果，在英文中雖然沒有直接的翻譯，卻也有類似的用法，船到橋頭自然直英文要怎麼說呢？可以用 "You will cross the bridge when you get to it." 來表示，另外還有一種類似的寫法是 "We will cross the bridge when we come to it."，意思為「當遇到橋，走過去就對了」，有表達出順其自然的處事態度。船到橋頭自然直在英文的口語上，也常使用 "Everything will work out in the end." 或 "Things will come right in the end." 來形容，亦即一切終將迎刃而解，常看好萊塢電影的觀眾應該多少有聽過，請看以下「船到橋頭自然直」英文例句：

- You will cross the bridge when you get to it.
- We will cross the bridge when we come to it.
- Everything will work out in the end.
- Things will come right in the end.

1-5 文化思考模式 (Cultural Thought Patterns)

　　美國學者Robert Kaplan於1966年指出：不同文化的族群有不同的思考模式，每一個文化有其獨特的書寫組織方式。爲了跨文化溝通有效，我們需要了解語言不同的文化思考模式。因爲這些不同的文化思考模式會影響其書面與口語表達的方式。

　　以下爲一個不同語言族群之不同文化模式的圖表，這個圖表並不是絕對的，但是可以作爲培養跨文化溝通的一個參考。

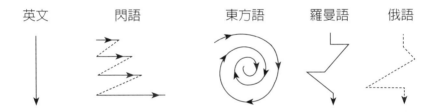

Taken from: Kaplan, R. (1966). Cultural thought patterns in intercultural education. *Language Learning*, pp.16, 1-20.

　　英文：（包括日耳曼語系的語言，如：德語、荷蘭語、挪威語、丹麥語與瑞典語）溝通很直接，直線性發展，不偏離主題。

　　閃語：（例如：阿拉伯語或希伯來語）思想以一系列平行的想法來表達，有正面的與反面的想法，同位語比附屬子句重要。

　　東方語：（亞洲語）溝通不直接，主題不直接提出，而是從各種不同的觀點考慮，旁敲側擊環繞主題。

　　羅曼語：（拉丁系語言，如：法語、義大利語、羅馬尼亞語與西班牙語）溝通時常脫離主題，介紹無關的素材，能夠增加溝通的豐富性也可以。

　　俄語：像羅曼語一樣，俄語的溝通時常脫離主題。離題可能包括一系列的平行想法。

　　由以上的圖表中，我們可以看出中文與英文的寫作方面有很大的差異，那就是英文的寫作修辭模式是直線發展的，而中文是迂迴的。所以當我們在閱讀英文文章時，只要能掌握第一段的thesis statement（主題陳述：即作者的主張、看法或意見），就可掌握全文的精髓，因為中間的段落，每一段的第一句有該段的中心思想（此為單一性〔unity〕原則），而最後一段作者會再複述其thesis statement（此為前後一致性原則〔coherence〕）。換言之，我們以作者寫作的方式來閱讀其文章，了解大意後再翻譯，可達事半功倍之效。以下列英文寫作模型表示：

英文寫作模型：五段式組織

介紹的段落 Introduction	1. 自己的立場（position） 2. 預告三個中心思想（3 main ideas） 3. 轉接句（transitional hook）
主體段落1 Body Paragraph 1	4. 主題句（topic sentence）（內含第一個中心思想 main idea） 5. 闡述句（supporting sentence） 6. 結論句（concluding sentence）
主體段落2 Body Paragraph 2	7. 主題句（內含第二個中心思想） 8. 闡述句 9. 結論句
主體段落3 Body Paragraph 3	10. 主題句（內含第三個中心思想） 11. 闡述句 12. 結論句
結論的段落 Conclusion	13. 複述三個中心思想（paraphrase 3 main ideas） 14. 重申自己的立場（restate position）

1-6 找英文句子大意的方法（Looking for the Main Idea in an English Sentence）

　　以下的萬用句型（generic sentence pattern）可以幫助讀者快速找到英文的主詞、動詞、受詞或補語。

　　英文一般皆有主詞（Subject）+ 動詞（Verb）的基本要素。大意一定是內容字（content words），如：主詞、動詞、受詞或補語，不會是功能字（function words）如：the/a/an或修飾語（adj.）、介詞片語、形容詞子句。

The	Prep. Phrase (of the...)
A + (Adj.) + N. (S.) +	Adj. Clause (who/which + S. V.) + V. (+ O./C.)
An	P.P. (-ed)
	V+ing

中英翻譯時應注意原則

　　基本上，中文是意合語言，句子比較短；而英文是形合語言，因常有後位修飾語（例如：以上句型介系詞片語、形容詞子句），所以句子比較長。

1. 增譯：有時需增加翻譯。
2. 減譯：有時需減少翻譯。
3. 詞性轉換：有時需詞性轉換，例如：名詞、動詞、形容詞、副詞、介詞需轉換。
4. 拆句：有時原文一句需拆成譯文二句、三句，甚至更多句。
5. 合併：有時原文二句、三句，甚至更多句需合併成一句譯文。
6. 主、被動句互換：有時需主動句與被動句互換。

7. 肯定、否定句互換：有時需肯定句與否定句互換。

8. 重組：有時翻譯時需重新組織整理，以符合中英文的文化思考模式、句法正確道地、慣用語法。

9. 綜合：總而言之，翻譯時，有時需要綜合運用以上的方法或技巧，以符合中英文的文化思考模式、句法正確道地，和慣用語法。

 斷句練習

1. 主詞 / 動詞 / 受詞（補語）一個單位間停頓

2. 連接詞 / 對等連接詞之前停頓（and/or/but, either...or..., both...and..., neither...nor, not only...but also..., ）

3. 修飾語 / 介系詞之前停頓（of the..., who/which/that, p.p., Ving）

4. 不定詞前停頓（to + V.）

5. 片語前後停頓（e.g., in order to, along with, as well as, tackle with... ）

6. 平行結構前後停頓（e.g., through identifying, analyzing and responding to potential risks）

練習 1

Over the eight years from 2006 up to last year, **407 people** in Yunlin County **died** in traffic accidents because they rode scooters without helmets or did not wear them properly, causing tragedies for countless broken families. (*Taipei Times*)

S. 407 people
V. died
Main idea: 407 people died in traffic accidents.

Over the eight years/ from 2006 up/ to last year, 407 people/ in Yunlin county /died/ in traffic accidents/ because they rode scooters/ without helmets /or did not wear them/ properly/, causing tragedies/ for countless broken families.

第
一
章

中
英
翻
譯
概
論

練習 2

Every **department** in the government **should have** a set of standard operating procedures for responding to emergency situations.

S. department
V. should have
Main idea: Every department should have a set of standard operating procedures.

Every department/ in the government/ should have/ a set of/ standard operating procedures/ for responding/ to emergency situations.

練習 3

With recommendation from a doctor, **people** who sit in an office for extended periods **should stand** for up to two hours a day to avoid illnesses and pains induced by extended sitting. (*Taipei Times*)

S. people
V. should stand
Main idea: People should stand for up to two hours a day.

With recommendation/ from a doctor/, people /who sit in an office/ for extended periods/ should stand/ for up to two hours a day/ to avoid illnesses/ and pains/ induced by extended sitting.

練習 4

The **way** a person types **can reveal** the state of their brain, according to a study that tracked keystrokes when the typist was alert or groggy (*Taipei Times*)

S. way

V. can reveal

Main idea: The way a person types can reveal the state of their brain.

The way/ a person types/ can reveal the state/ of their brain/, according to a study/ that tracked keystrokes/ when the typist/ was alert/ or groggy.

練習 5

A rare Siberian white **crane** that arrived alone in the Cingshuei wetlands in New Taipei's Jinshan District in December last year **is seen** in a photo taken in April. (*Taipei Times*)

S. crane

V. is seen

Main idea: A white crane is seen in a photo.

A rare Siberian white crane/ that arrived alone/ in the Cingshuei wetlands/ in New Taipei's Jinshan District/ in December/ last year is seen/ in a photo/ taken in April.

練習 6

According to police statistics, the **number** of deaths caused by failure to wear crash helmets in line with the regulations **fell** from 47 the year before last to 33 last year, suggesting that this policy has been quite effective. (*Taipei Times*)

S. number

V. fell

Main idea: The number of deaths fell from 47 the year before last to 33 last year.

According to police statistics/, the number of deaths/ caused by failure/ to wear crash helmets/ in line with the regulations/ fell from 47/ the year before last/ to 33 last year/, suggesting/ that this policy/ has been quite effective.

 練習 7

A **sand sculpture** portraying characters from the One Piece manga series **is pictured** at the Fulong International Sand Sculpture Art Festival in Keelung on May 4, 2013. (*Taipei Times*)

S. sand sculpture
V. is pictured
Main idea: A sand sculpture is pictured.

A sand sculpture/ portraying characters/ from the One Piece manga series/ is pictured/ at the Fulong International Sand Sculpture Art Festival/ in Keelung/ on May 4/, 2013.

練習 8

過去分詞構句，表被動
Filled with fascinating insights, humorous observations, and simple strategies that you can apply to any situation, **this intriguing book will enrich** your communication with and understanding of others—as well as yourself. (Pease & Pease, 2008)

S. this book
V. will enrich
Main idea: This book will enrich your communication with and understanding of others.

Filled with fascinating insights/, humorous observations/, and simple strategies/ that you can apply/ to any situation, this intriguing book/ will enrich your communication with/ and understanding of others/–as well as yourself.

練習9

過去分詞構句，表被動

Scared by the sudden commotion, **the Siberian white crane was frightened** from its natural habitat and flew off to another area. (*Taipei Times*)

S. crane
V. was frightened
Main idea: The white crane was frightened.

Scared/ by the sudden commotion/, the Siberian white crane/ was frightened/ from its natural habitat/ and flew off to another area.

練習10

現在分詞構句，表主動

Drawing upon more than thirty years in the field, as well as cutting-edge research from evolutionary biology, psychology, and medical technologies that demonstrate what happens in the brain, **the authors examine** each component of body language and give you the basic vocabulary to read attitudes and emotions through behavior.

S. the authors
V. examine
Main idea: The authors examine each component of body language and give you the basic vocabulary...

Drawing upon more than thirty years/ in the field/, as well as cutting-edge research/ from evolutionary biology/, psychology/, and medical technologies/ that demonstrate/ what happens/ in the brain, the authors/ examine each component/ of body language/ and give you the basic vocabulary/ to read attitudes/ and emotions/ through behavior.

練習11

獨立分詞構句：

Weather permitting, we will go mountain climbing next Monday.

慣用語：Generally speaking... 一般來說……

Frankly speaking... 坦白說……

Strictly speaking... 嚴格地說

Roughly speaking... 大約地說

Judging from (by)... 由……判斷……

Considering... 考慮到……

Concerning... 關於……

Speaking of... 說到……

Seeing that... 既然……

Provided that... 假如……

第二章　中英翻譯的三個基本方法與轉換法的六個技巧

2-1 前 言（Preface）

　　由於中文和英文的句法結構不同，所以中翻英或英翻中時，譯者常常需要彈性地運用方法與技巧。譯者除了需具備優秀的語言能力，還需要熟悉翻譯的方法與技巧。一般而言，中英翻譯有三個基本方法：（1）增加法（Adding Approach）；（2）減少法（Subtracting Approach）；（3）轉換法（Transforming Approach）。具體而言，中英翻譯轉換法有六個技巧：（1）改變技巧（Changing Skill）；（2）拆句技巧（Splitting Skill）；（3）合併技巧（Combining Skill）；（4）肯定句否定句交換技巧（Affirmative/Negative Switching Skill）；（5）重組技巧（Restructuring Skill）；（6）綜合技巧（Synthesizing Skill）。 編者認為，以上所提到的三個方法和六個技巧是互補的而非互相獨立的，而且翻譯人員在翻譯時往往需要同時使用兩個以上的方法與技巧。編者認為，中英文翻譯以「信、達、雅」為指導方針，英文翻譯成中文時，以通順暢達為原則；而中文翻譯成英文時，以合乎英文句法為原則。總之，不論是英翻中或是中翻英，譯文（translated language）必須掌握原文（source language）的涵義，符合譯文的文化思考模式、句法正確道地、慣用語法。

2-2 中英翻譯的三個基本方法（Three Fundamental Approaches to Chinese-English Translation）

（一）增加法（Adding Approach）

　　第一個基本方法是「增加法」。「增加法」指的就是在翻譯時，掌握原文（source language）的涵義，根據譯文（translated language）的文化思考模式（cultural thought patterns）、句法正確道地（syntactic correctness and authenticity）、慣用語法（common expressions），增加一些字、片語或句子。雖然這些字、片語或句子在原文中並沒有出現，但是增加這些字、片語或句子可使譯文句法正確，語意更明白流暢，以便忠實地傳達原文的意思（「信」），充分地傳達原文的涵義（「達」），優雅地傳達原文的意境（「雅」）。總之，「增加法」就是增加一些字、片語或句子，以符合譯文的語法與句法，使語意更明白流暢。

 例1

【原文】：根據天氣預報，冷鋒正向臺灣移動。

【譯文】：According to **the** weather forecast, **a** cold front is moving toward Taiwan.

【解析】：在中文裡「天氣預報」，在英文裡要加入"the"。另外，在中文裡「冷鋒」，在英文裡要加入"a"。

冷鋒 cold front

寒流 cold current; cold snap

 例2

【原文】：公園裡有6、7個銀髮族在打太極拳。

【譯文】：There are six **or** seven senior citizens practicing Chinese shadow boxing in **the** park.

【解析】：在中文裡出現「6、7個」銀髮族，但在英文裡要加入"or"。另外，在中文裡「公園裡」，在英文裡要加入"the"。

銀髮族 seniors, senior citizens

太極拳 Chinese shadow boxing; Taijiquan

例3

【原文】：在臺灣墾丁浮潛蠻好玩的。

【譯文】：**It** is quite interesting to **go** snorkeling at Kenting in Taiwan.

【解析】：在中文裡出現「蠻好玩的」，但在英文裡要加入 "It"。另外，在中文裡出現「浮潛」，在英文裡要加入 "go"。

浮潛 go snorkeling; snorkel diving

深潛 scuba diving

 例4

【原文】：她心情很好。

【譯文】：She is **in a** good mood.

【解析】：在中文裡出現「心情」，但在英文裡要加入 "a"。另外，在英文裡要加入 "in"。

 例5

【原文】：彼得似乎喜歡韓語。

【譯文】：Peter seems to be fond of **learning** Korean.

【解析】：在中文裡出現「韓語」，但在英文裡要加入 "learning"。

 例6

【原文】：你們能不能小聲點啊？

【譯文】：Could you guys keep **it** down in there?

Could you guys keep **your voices** down in there?

【解析】：在中文裡出現「小聲」，但在英文裡要加入 "it" 或 "your voices"。另外，在英文裡可以加入 "there" 或 "in there"。

【原文】：許多學者主張英文已成為國際語言，最好學好。

【譯文】：（1）Many scholars take the position that English has become **the** international language. **We** had better master it.

（2）Many scholars advocate that English has become **the** international language; **we** had better master it.

（3）It is many scholars' contention that English has become **the** international language, so **we** had better master it.

【解析】：雖然中文裡並沒有明顯指出「一種」，冠詞 "a" 或 "the" 必須加在 "language" 或其他普通名詞之前。另外，在中文裡只有「最好學好」並沒有出現「我們」，但是加上主詞 "we" 可使英文句法結構正確而語意更清楚，最後面加上 "it"。最後，中文看起來是一個句子，但是翻譯成英文時要注意句法，避免造成英文所謂的 run-on sentences。

【註解】：run-on sentences 連寫句（指兩個主句之間不用連接詞或錯用標點的句子）

例子：Nothing is fixed in this world; everything is relative. 在這個世界上沒有什麼東西是固定不變的；一切都是相對的。

【原文】：The town was destroyed by the typhoon.

【譯文】：**整座**城鎮被颱風毀滅了。

【解析】：增加形容詞「整座的」。

實用中英翻譯法

例9

【原文】：The story has been watered down.

【譯文】：這個故事的**生動性**已被削弱了。

【解析】：增加名詞「生動性」。

 例10

【原文】：I don't much care for television.

【譯文】：我不太喜歡**看**電視。

【解析】：增加動詞「看」。

 例11

【原文】：The snow melted away at noon.

【譯文】：中午雪**漸漸地**融化了。

【解析】：增加副詞「漸漸地」。

 例12

【原文】：新疆白天與黑夜的溫差是攝氏30度。

【譯文】：The difference **in** temperature **between** the day and the night in Xinjiang is thirty degrees celcius (centigrade).

【解析】：增加介系詞 "in"、"between"。

攝氏的 celcius [`sɛlsɪəs]

華氏的 fahrenheit [`færən͵haɪt]

 例13

【原文】：你能區分猿和猴嗎？

【譯文】：Can you tell the difference **between** an ape and a monkey?

【解析】：增加介系詞 "between"。

區分 tell the difference; make a distinction

例14

【原文】：While I like the color of the evening dress, I do not like its style.

【譯文】：雖然我喜歡這件晚禮服的顏色，**但是我不喜歡它的樣式**。

【解析】：增加連接詞「但是」。

例15

【原文】：The general manager is concerned at the decline in the revenues of the company.

【譯文】：總經理對公司總收入的減少**甚為**關注。

【解析】：增譯「甚為」。

general manager, managing director 總經理

decline; drop; fall; decrease; downturn; worsening 減少

例16

【原文】：We went for a drive in the afternoon.

【譯文】：我們下午開車**出去兜風**。

【解析】：增加「出去兜風」。

例17

【原文】：如果你可以幫忙我的話，我會很感激。

【譯文】：I would appreciate **it** if you could do me a favor.

【解析】：增加 "it"。

（二）減少法（Subtracting Approach）

第二個基本方法是「減少法」。與增加法相反，減少法指的就是在翻譯時，掌握原文的涵義，在譯文中減少一些字、片語或句子，以符合目標語或譯文之文化思考模式、句法正確道地和慣用語法。雖然

實用中英翻譯法

這些字、片語或句子在原文中有出現，但是減少這些字、片語或句子可使譯文句法正確，語意更明白流暢，以便忠實地傳達原文的意思（「信」），充分地傳達原文的涵義（「達」），優雅地傳達原文的意境（「雅」）。總之，「減少法」就是減少一些字、片語或句子，以符合譯文的語法與句法，使語意更清楚順暢。

 例1

【原文】：他**雖然**身體不舒服，**但**仍努力工作。

【譯文】：**Although** he was under the weather, he worked hard.

He was under the weather, **but** he worked hard.

【解析】：第一句英文裡的 "but" 與第二句英文裡的 "Although" 不需要翻譯出來。換言之，"Although" 和 "but" 都是連接詞，在一個英文句子裡只能用其中一個連接詞。

 例2

【原文】：**因為**她很窮，**所以**她必須打工繳學費。

【譯文】：She is poor, **so** she needs to work part time for her tuition.

Because she is poor, she needs to work part time for her tuition.

【解析】：第一句英文裡的 "so" 與第二句英文裡的 "because" 不需要翻譯出來。換言之，"so" 和 "because" 都是連接詞，在一個英文句子裡只能用其中一個連接詞。

 例3

【原文】：**It** is important to be punctual.

【譯文】：守時很重要。

【解析】：在中文裡，英文 "it" 不需要翻譯出來。

例4

【原文】：Simplified Chinese characters are only **apparently** "simpler". In fact, they destroy the underlying logic of the system.

【譯文】：簡體字把一個字變簡單，卻破壞了造字系統和邏輯。

【解析】：在中文裡，"apparently" 沒有翻譯出來。

例5

【原文】：This is a really helpful reference book to us **because** it explains everything about translation in detail.

【譯文】：這一本參考書對我們很有幫助，有關翻譯的事項都說明地很詳細。

【解析】：在中文裡，"because" 不需要翻譯出來。

例6

【原文】：Smoking is not permitted **in** the National Palace Museum.

【譯文】：國立故宮博物院裡禁止抽菸。

【解析】：在中文裡，"in" 不需翻譯出來。

例7

【原文】：**I** wish you a happy birthday.

【譯文】：祝你生日快樂。

【解析】：減譯主詞 "I"。

祝你生日快樂不能翻譯為 I wish you <u>have</u> a happy birthday.

例8

【原文】：**We** wish you a merry Christmas.

【譯文】：祝你聖誕快樂。

【解析】：減譯主詞 "We"。

祝你聖誕快樂不能翻譯爲 We wish you have a merry Christmas.

 例9

【原文】：**Between** work and studies Matthew has no time left.

【譯文】：工作和學習使馬修無暇他顧。

【解析】：減譯介系詞 "Between"。

 例10

【原文】：因爲他們的棒球教練退休了，**因此**我們教練兩年前接管了他們的球隊。

【譯文】：**Because** their baseball coach retired, our coach took over their team two years ago.

【解析】：減譯連接詞「因此」。

 例11

【原文】：吉米及比利1975年被徵召至海軍服役。

【譯文】：Jimmy and Billy were enlisted in the navy in 1975.

【解析】：減譯動詞「服役」。

（三）轉換法（Transforming Approach）

　　第三個基本方法是「轉換法」，轉換法就是在翻譯時，掌握原文的涵義，根據譯文的文化思考模式、句法正確道地、慣用語法，譯文對原文中的詞類、語態或句型加以轉換。轉換這些詞類、語態或句型可使譯文句法正確，語意更明白流暢，以便忠實地傳達原文的意思

（「信」），充分地傳達原文的涵義（「達」），優雅地傳達原文的意境（「雅」）。總之，由於中文和英文的語法與句法不同，所以中翻英或英翻中時，常常需要轉換詞類、語態或句型。

 例1

【原文】：約翰興高采烈地喝完了柳橙汁。

【譯文】：John **finished** his orange juice **in good spirits**.

【解析】：在中文裡出現「喝完了」，但在英文裡翻成 "finished"。另外，在中文裡出現「興高采烈地」，在英文裡可翻成 "in good spirits"。

無精打采地 in very low spirits

 例2

【原文】：因為可能會有隨堂考，所以馬可認眞讀書。

【譯文】：Mark studied hard because of the **possibility** of a pop quiz.

【解析】：在中文裡出現「可能」，但在英文裡可轉換成名詞 "possibility"。

 例3

【原文】：我親眼目睹了他創新的企業家精神。

【譯文】：I witnessed the **innovation** of his entreprenership.

【解析】：在英文裡，「創新的」轉譯成名詞 "innovation"。

 例4

【原文】：經過了激烈的討價還價，雙方終於達成協議。

【譯文】：After **a lot of** haggling, the two sides reached an agreement eventually.

【解析】：在英文裡，「激烈的」轉譯成 "a lot of"。

終於 in the end; finally; eventually; ultimately

例5

【原文】：怎樣才能縮小貧富之間的差距？

【譯文】：How can we **bridge the gap** between rich and poor?

【解析】：在英文裡，「縮小差距」轉譯成 "bridge the gap"。

 例6

【原文】：政府試圖在這一問題上保持低姿態。

【譯文】：The government tried to **keep a low profile** on this issue.

【解析】：在英文裡，「保持低姿態」轉譯成 "keep a low pro-file"。

保持低調；保持低姿態 keep a low profile

 例7

【原文】：Think twice before you resign. If you resign now, you will **burn** your **bridges**.

【譯文】：你對辭職一事須三思。現在辭職就會斷自己的後路。

【解析】：中文「如果」不需翻譯出來。

burn the bridge/boat 斷後路

 例8

【原文】：The comments have been **watered down** in order not to offend anyone.

【譯文】：這些批評意見已修改得緩和些以免得罪人。

【解析】：water down 減弱（某事物的作用）；刪改；緩和

 例9

【原文】：The teacher has to **water down** the course requirement for a low-achieving class.

第二章　中英翻譯的三個基本方法與轉換法的六個技巧

【譯文】：教師不得不降低課程的要求，以適應低成就的班級。

【解析】：water down 降低要求

例10

【原文】：It is not easy to **strike a balance** between your job and your family.

【譯文】：你的工作與家庭之間，要取得平衡點很不容易。

【解析】：strike a balance 取得平衡點

例11

【原文】：It is difficult for people to **strike the right balance** between justice and expediency.

【譯文】：人們在公正與利己之間很難兩全。

【解析】：strike the right balance 兩全

例12

【原文】：Many investors **are attracted** to opportunities in emerging markets.

【譯文】：新興市場帶來的機會吸引許多投資人。

【解析】：英文原句爲被動句，翻譯時轉譯爲主動句。

例13

【原文】：My parents are **in agreement** on what color to paint the wall of the living room.

【譯文】：我父母對於用什麼顏色漆客廳的牆壁意見一致。

【解析】："in agreement" 名詞轉譯爲動詞「意見一致」。

例14

【原文】：I have a very high **regard** for your medical expertise.

【譯文】：我非常器重你的醫學專門知識。

【解析】："regard" 名詞轉譯為動詞「器重」。

expertise 專門知識；專長

例15

【原文】：He **is** generally **thought of as** one of the best students in the class.

【譯文】：大家都認為他是班上最好的學生之一。

【解析】：被動語態轉譯為主動語態。

主動：視……為……：regard...as... = take...as... = think of...as... = look on/upon...as... = view...as... = see...as...

被動：被視為……：be regarded as... = be taken as..., be thought of as... = be looked on/upon as... = be viewed as... = be seen as...

例16

【原文】：There is **a general belief** that the company is in financial difficulties.

【譯文】：一般意見認為該公司財政困難。

【解析】：名詞 "a general belief" 轉譯為主詞加動詞「一般意見認為」。

There is a general belief that... 一般意見認為……

It is our general belief that... 我們普遍認為……

in fianancial trouble 財務陷入困境

in severe financial trouble 財務陷入嚴重困境

in fianancial difficulties 財政困難

adj. + belief: absolute, deep-seated, deeply held, fervent, firm, passionate, profound, strong, strongly held, un-

第二章 中英翻譯的三個基本方法與轉換法的六個技巧

039

shakeable, genuine, honest, sincere, entrenched, fanatical, common, commonly held, general, popular, widely held, widespread, growing, long-held, long-standing

實用中英翻譯法

例17

【原文】：Children's bad behavior is often a **reflection** on their parents.

【譯文】：小孩的壞品行常常有損父母的名譽。

【解析】：名詞 "reflection" 轉譯為動詞「有損……的名譽」。

例18

【原文】：On **reflection**, she decided to follow your advice.

【譯文】：她重新考慮後，決定聽你的勸告。

【解析】：名詞 "reflection" 轉譯為動詞「考慮」。"advice" 為不可數名詞不加 s，如："some advice, a piece of advice"。

decided; made up someone's mind 決定

follow someone's advice 聽某人的勸告

act on someone's advice 按某人的勸告行事

例19

【原文】：**Relative** to its size, the city is densely populated.

【譯文】：與它的面積相比，這座城市人口密度很高。

【解析】：relative [ˋrɛlətɪv] 形容詞 "relative" 轉譯為動詞「與……相比」。

be densely populated 人口密度高

a densely populated country 人口密度高的國家

sparsely populated 人口極為稀少

a sparsely populated country 人口極為稀少的國家

例20

【原文】：**I wasn't born yesterday**.

【譯文】：我又不是3歲小孩。

【解析】：句子轉譯。

例21

【原文】：I will **thank** you to turn on the lights.

【譯文】：請你把電燈打開。

【解析】："thank" 轉譯成「請」。另外，thank 用於 will 之後，表示客氣的請求。

例22

【原文】：He could not **account for** his absence from school.

【譯文】：他無法說清楚為什麼曠課。

【解析】：account for 解釋，說明；對……負責

absent from school 轉譯為「曠課」。

例23

【原文】：Millions of **fans follow** the TV soap opera devotedly.

【譯文】：數百萬觀眾非常忠實地收看這部電視連續劇。

【解析】："fans" 翻譯為「觀眾」；"follow" 翻譯為「收看」。

soap opera 肥皂劇（以家庭問題為題材的廣播或電視連續劇）

例24

【原文】：給你點顏色瞧瞧。

【譯文】：I'll show you **who the boss is**.

【解析】：轉譯整個句子。

第二章　中英翻譯的三個基本方法與轉換法的六個技巧

例25

【原文】：此地區人山人海。

【譯文】：This area is **crowded with people**.

【解析】：轉譯整個句子。

例26

【原文】：我們景況相同。

【譯文】：We are **in the same boat**.

【解析】：轉譯整個句子。

2-3 中英翻譯轉換法的六個技巧（Six Skills in the Transforming Approach to Chinese-English Translation）

（一）改變技巧（Changing Skill）

　　第一個技巧就是改變技巧，改變技巧就是掌握原文的涵義，根據譯文的文化思考模式、句法正確道地和慣用語法，來改變原文中的**詞類、語態**和**句型**。

1. 詞類改變

例1

【原文】：The man **impressed** her very unfavorably.

【譯文】：這位男士給她的**印象**極差。

【解析】：動詞 "impressed" 改變成名詞「印象」。

例2

【原文】：Her piano performance **impressed** the audience very **favorably**.

【譯文】：她的鋼琴演奏留給聽眾很好的印象。

【解析】：動詞 "impressed" 改變成名詞「印象」；副詞 "favorably" 改變成形容詞「很好的」。

例3

【原文】：Many people **responded** favorably to the project.

【譯文】：許多人的反應是贊同該企劃。

【解析】：動詞 "responded" 改變成名詞「反應」。

例4

【原文】：I am all **in favor of** your opinions.

【譯文】：我完全贊同你的意見。

【解析】：介詞片語 "in favor of " 改變成動詞「贊同」。

例5

【原文】：他們都樂於接受我們的提議。

【譯文】：They are all **agreeable** to our suggestions.

【解析】：動詞「接受」改變為形容詞 "agreeable"。

例6

【原文】：I have a very high **regard** for your expertise.

【譯文】：我非常器重你的專業。

【解析】："regard" 名詞改變為動詞「器重」。

例7

【原文】：Please give my best **regards** to your parents.

【譯文】：請代我向您的雙親問好。

【解析】："regards" 名詞改變為動詞「問好」。

例8

【原文】：I'm not **equal** to the mission.

【譯文】：我不能**勝任**這項任務。

【解析】："equal" 形容詞改變為動詞「勝任」。

例9

【原文】：His view was **seconded** by many experts.

【譯文】：他的觀點受到許多專家的**支持**。

【解析】："seconded" 動詞改變為名詞「支持」。

例10

【原文】：He failed completely in the **performance** of his duty.

【譯文】：他完全沒有**履行**他的職責。

【解析】：名詞 "performance" 改變為動詞「履行」。

例11

【原文】：He **made an attempt** on the world record.

【譯文】：他**試圖打破**世界紀錄。

【解析】：make an attempt 試圖打破

例12

【原文】：Only a few people can have **access** to the full facts of the case.

【譯文】：只有少數幾個人能**看到**有關該案全部事實的資料。

【解析】：名詞 "access" 改變為動詞「看到」。

例13

【原文】：We are **with** you there.

【譯文】：在那一點上我們站在你這一邊。

實用中英翻譯法

【解析】：介系詞 "with" 改變爲動詞「站在……一邊；贊成」。

例14

【原文】：What can you **conclude** from these observations?

【譯文】：你從這些觀察中能得出什麼結論？

【解析】："conclude" 動詞改變爲名詞「結論」。

例15

【原文】：The girl has **progressed** in her studies.

【譯文】：這女孩學習方面有進步。

【解析】：動詞 "progressed" 改變爲名詞「進步」。

例16

【原文】：Taipei's Xinyi District **is home to** many quality clothing stores.

【譯文】：臺北的信義區有許多高級的服飾店。

【解析】："is home to" 改變爲「有」。

high-end; high-class; quality 高級的

例17

【原文】：My father does not have much **belief** in doctors of traditional Chinese medicine.

【譯文】：我父親不太相信中醫。

【解析】：名詞 "belief" 改變爲動詞「相信」。

Traditional Chinese Medicine（TCM）傳統中醫

例18

【原文】：How can he get the promotion **when** his boss dislikes him?

【譯文】：既然上司不喜歡他，那他怎麼會獲得晉升呢？

【解析】："when" 翻譯爲「既然」。

例19

【原文】：Robert is deeply **appreciative** of your help.

【譯文】：羅伯特對你的幫助深表感激。

【解析】："appreciative" 形容詞翻譯爲名詞「感激」。

2. 語態改變

例1

【原文】：Smoking **is prohibited** in the office building.

【譯文】：辦公大樓禁止抽菸。

【解析】：被動語態轉變成主動語態。

例2

【原文】：這片海灘禁止游泳。

【譯文】：Swimming **is not allowed** at this beach.

【解析】：主動語態轉變成被動語態。

准許：同意 allowed; permitted

例3

【原文】：**Several attempts have been made** to access your bank account with incorrect username and password.

【譯文】：已經有人好幾次以不正確的使用者名稱與密碼，**試圖進入**使用你的銀行帳戶。

【解析】：被動語態轉變成主動語態。

例4

【原文】：I **was** much **moved** by her life story.

【譯文】：她的人生故事深深**打動**了我。

【解析】：被動語態轉變成主動語態。

be much/very much moved/touched/impressed 深受感動

例5

【原文】：All my proposals **were granted**.

【譯文】：我所有的提案全都得到許可。

【解析】：被動語態轉變成主動語態。

例6

【原文】：Remarkable advances **have been made** in space science.

【譯文】：太空科學已有了長足的發展。

【解析】：被動語態轉譯成主動語態。

advances/progress 搭配詞

（1）adj. + advances: big, considerable, dramatic, enormous, great, spectacular, substantial, tremendous, important, major, notable, remarkable, significant, rapid, steady

（2）adj. + progress: considerable, dramatic, encouraging, excellent, genuine, good, great, impressive, real, remarkable, significant, substantial, fast, rapid, swift, inexorable, slow, stately

例7

【原文】：In the interest of safety, **no smoking is permitted** here.

【譯文】：為了安全，這裡**嚴禁吸菸**。

【解析】：被動語態轉譯成主動語態。

例8

【原文】：There are a lot of difficulties that have **to be overcome**.

【譯文】：有許多困難**必須克服**。

【解析】：被動語態轉譯成主動語態。

3. 句型改變

例1

【原文】：成功必須有積極的態度。

【譯文】：Positive attitude **is essential to** success.

【解析】：句子轉換。

例2

【原文】：**Privatization is considered to be beneficial** in that it promotes competition.

【譯文】：私有化的優點在於能促進相互競爭。

【解析】：in that = in the sense that 基於……的理由；因為
privatization [ˌpraɪvətaɪˋzeʃən] 私有化；非國營化
（將國營企業轉為民營）

例3

【原文】：Some people like fatty meat, **whereas** others hate it.

【譯文】：有些人喜歡肥肉，有些人卻不喜歡。

【解析】：whereas = while「而」沒有翻出來。

例4

【原文】：I **don't think** they would permit this.

【譯文】：我想他們不會准許這件事。

【解析】："I don't think" 為「我想……不會」。

例5

【原文】：Boys and girls **are given the opportunity** to get to know each other and to learn to get along with each other from their earlier years.

【譯文】：男女生之間**有機會**了解彼此，有機會從人生的早期便開始學習如何相處。

【解析】："are given the opportunity" 中文翻成「有機會」，另
　　　　起一句「有機會」。

例6

【原文】：女科學家獎一方面肯定卓然有成的女性研究者，**另一**
　　　　方面也鼓勵嶄露頭角的後進。（《臺灣光華雜誌》）

【譯文】：The awards for women in science recognize the outstand-
　　　　ing achievements of established female researchers, **while**
　　　　also encouraging up-and-comers. (*Taiwan Panorama*)

【解析】：中文「另一方面」翻成 "while"。

例7

【原文】：她對錢的看法是：來得容易去得快。

【譯文】：Her **attitude** toward money is easy come easy go.

【解析】：中文為二個句子，而英文為一個句子。
　　　　中文「看法」英文譯為 "attitude"。

例8

【原文】：He traveled **extensively** to **escape from boredom**.

【譯文】：他到處旅遊以解煩悶。

【解析】："extensively" 改譯為「到處」，"to escape from bore-
　　　　dom" 改譯為「以解煩悶」。

例9

【原文】：你可以在圖書館裡找到這本書。

【譯文】：This book is available in the library.

【解析】：受詞譯為主詞。

例10

【原文】：藥品應放在兒童不容易拿到的安全的地方。

【譯文】：Medicine should be kept in a secure place so that it is not **accessible** to children.

【解析】：主詞兒童譯為受詞。

例11

【原文】：她突然想到一個主意。

【譯文】：Suddenly an idea **occurred to** her.

Suddenly an idea **struck** her.

Suddenly an idea **crossed** her **mind**.

【解析】：受詞譯為主詞。

例12

【原文】：**Seafood** doesn't agree with **me**.

【譯文】：我不適宜吃海鮮。

【解析】：受詞譯為主詞。

例13

【原文】：What should I do to **obtain a deeper understanding** of God's love?

【譯文】：我該怎麼做才能深入了解神的愛？

【解析】：obtain a deeper understanding 深入了解

例14

【原文】：She **has a great curiosity about** how space shuttle travels.

【譯文】：她對太空梭的旅行充滿好奇。

【解析】：have a great curiosity about 對……充滿好奇

例15

【原文】：He danced with the indigenous people **at the invitation of** the tour guide.

【譯文】：他受導遊的**邀請**與原住民共舞。

【解析】：at the invitation of 受……的邀請

例16

【原文】：蓋金字塔需要龐大的人力。

【譯文】：You need a lot of manpower **to build a pyramid**.

【解析】：句子轉變。

例17

【原文】：船到橋頭自然直。

【譯文】：Things will come right in the end.
　　　　　You will **cross the bridge** when you get to it.

【解析】：第一句譯文中並未將「船」與「橋頭」直譯出來；
　　　　　而第二句譯文中並未將「船」與「直」直譯出來。

例18

【原文】：Finally the real challenge **came home to** us.

【譯文】：最終我們完全清楚了真正的挑戰。

【解析】："the real challenge" 轉變為受詞。
　　　　　come home to sb. 某人完全領會；某人清楚地理解

例19

【原文】：Your e-mail address has **slipped my mind**.

【譯文】：你的電子郵件地址我忘了。

【解析】："slipped my mind" 轉譯為「我忘了」。

（二）拆句技巧（Splitting Skill）

第二個技巧就是拆句技巧，拆句技巧就是掌握原文的涵義，根據譯文的文化思考模式、句法正確道地和慣用語法，來對原文中的單字、片語、句子加以拆句。

1. 單字拆句

例1

【原文】：At that moment she was **surprisingly** attractive.

【譯文】：令人驚訝地，她當時很嫵媚動人。

【解析】："surprisingly" 單字拆句為「令人驚訝地」。

例2

【原文】：The great complexity of the machine **prohibits** its wide-spread application.

【譯文】：這機器極為複雜，很難普及應用。

【解析】："prohibit" 單字拆句為「很難」。

2. 片語拆句

例1

【原文】：I tried to persuade her **in vain**.

【譯文】：我想說服她，但是枉然。

【解析】："in vain" 片語拆句為「枉然」。

to convince sb. of sth.; persuade 使某人確信；使某人信服；說服某人

例2

【原文】：He tried but **in vain**.

【譯文】：他試過，但徒勞無功。

【解析】："in vain" 片語拆句為「徒勞無功」。

例3

【原文】：He was **so** angry **that** he almost lost control.

【譯文】：他非常生氣，以致於近乎失控。

【解析】："so...that..." 片語拆句爲「如此（非常）……，以致於……」。

 例4

【原文】：Nothing more was heard from her **so that** we began to wonder if she disappeared.

【譯文】：再也沒聽到她的消息，**因此**我們開始懷疑她是否失蹤了。

【解析】："so that" 片語拆句爲「結果」、「以致」、「因此」。

 例5

【原文】：John is brilliant, **so much so that** he can understand the quantum theory.

【譯文】：約翰很聰明，**聰明到**可以理解量子理論。

【解析】：so much so that... 到如此程度以至於……。

 例6

【原文】：He'll be **angry to find that** nothing has been completed.

【譯文】：看到什麼也沒有完成，他準會生氣。

【解析】：be angry to find that 因爲……而生氣。

 例7

【原文】：He succeeded **in the face of** a lot of difficulties.

【譯文】：儘管遭遇許多困難，他還是成功了。

【解析】："in the face of" 片語拆句爲「遭遇」面對。

第二章　中英翻譯的三個基本方法與轉換法的六個技巧

例8

【原文】：I dabbled in painting for a full two years **before giving up**.

【譯文】：我試著畫畫滿兩年，*之後就放棄了*。

【解析】："before giving up" 拆句爲「之後就放棄了」。

例9

【原文】：Great was his joy **on hearing this good news**.

【譯文】：*聽到這件好消息*，他大喜過望。

【解析】："on hearing this good news" 拆句爲「聽到這件好消息」。

例10

【原文】：They confused me **by their conflicting opinions**.

【譯文】：*他們的意見相互矛盾*，把我弄糊塗了。

【解析】："by their conflicting opinions" 拆句爲「他們的意見相互矛盾」。

例11

【原文】：It is not the bank's policy to **deduct interest from withdrawals**.

【譯文】：*提款需扣除利息*，這並非是本銀行的政策。

【解析】："to deduct interest from withdrawals" 爲不定詞片語拆句「提款需扣除利息」。

3. 句子拆句

例1

【原文】：Linsanity has proven a superstar in Asia, where he is even more popular than in his home country, the United States.

【譯文】：林書豪已證明他在亞洲是一個超級巨星，而且在亞洲比在祖國──美國，更受歡迎。

【解析】：一句拆成三句。

 例2

【原文】：Researchers have established that when people are mentally engaged, biochemical changes occur in the brain that allow it to act more effectively in cognitive areas such as attention and memory.

【譯文】：研究人員證實：人們在動腦筋時，頭腦會產生很多的變化，使頭腦在注意力和記憶力這類認知領域中更有效地活動。

【解析】：一句拆成三句。

（三）合併技巧（Combining Skill）

第三個技巧就是合併技巧，合併技巧就是掌握原文的涵義，根據譯文的文化思考模式、句法正確道地和慣用語法，來對原文中的詞類、句型加以合併。

 例1

【原文】：He studied for the test. He felt confident.

【譯文】：為考試而讀書增加了他的信心。

【解析】：合併二個英文句子譯成一個中文句子。

 例2

【原文】：前人種樹，後人乘涼。──華倫‧巴菲特

【譯文】：Someone's sitting in the shade today **because** someone planted a tree a long time ago. ──Warrcn Buffett

【解析】：合併二個中文句子譯成一句英文。

例3

【原文】：少壯不努力，老大徒傷悲。

【譯文】：He who does not work hard in youth will be sorry in vain **when old**.

【解析】：合併二個中文句子譯成一句英文。

凡是……的人 Those who...；People who...；He who（三單動詞）；One who（三單動詞）

例4

【原文】：When you stand like that, you look like a statue.

【譯文】：你站那個樣子活像個雕像。

【解析】：合併二個英文句子（副詞子句與主句）譯成一句中文。

（四）肯定句否定句交換技巧（Affirmative/Negative Switching Skill）

第四個技巧就是肯定句否定句交換技巧，肯定句否定句交換技巧就是掌握原文的涵義，根據譯文的文化思考模式、句法正確道地和慣用語法，來對原文中的肯定否定句型加以轉換。

例1

【原文】：Her name **escapes me**.

【譯文】：我記不起她的名字了。

【解析】：肯定句譯為否定句。

例2

【原文】：I **can't** agree with you **more**.

【譯文】：我非常同意你的看法（或說法）。

【解析】：否定句譯為肯定句。

例3

【原文】：I **can't** thank you **enough**.

【譯文】：我對你真是感激不盡。

【解析】：否定句譯為肯定句。

例4

【原文】：That lecture on neuroscience was **above me**.

【譯文】：那場神經科學的演講我聽不懂。

【解析】：肯定句譯為否定句。

例5

【原文】：What a performance!

【譯文】：真沒教養！

【解析】：肯定句譯為否定句。

（五）重組技巧（Restructuring Skill）

　　第五個技巧就是重組技巧，重組技巧就是掌握原文的涵義，根據譯文的文化思考模式、句法正確道地和慣用語法，來對原文中的**詞類、語序和句型**加以重組。

例1

【原文】：John has recently made rapid strides toward his goal of mastering Chinese.

【譯文】：約翰最近朝向學好中文的目標突飛猛進。

【解析】：先翻譯「約翰最近」，然後翻譯「朝向學好中文的目標」，最後翻譯「突飛猛進」。

例2

【原文】：Don't judge each day by the harvest you reap, but by the seeds you plant. ——Robert Louis Steveenson

【譯文】：不要以所得的收穫，而是所撒的種子來評斷每一
天。——英國作家羅伯特‧路易斯‧史蒂文生

【解析】：最後翻譯「來評斷每一天」。

例3

【原文】：Mainland China has vast sums of money to spend, but
Taiwan can establish a strong position thanks to three
factors: our foothold in overseas Chinese communities,
our use of traditional characters, and our educational in-
novativeness. (*Taiwan Panorama*)

【譯文】：中國大陸的人海、錢海戰術很強大，但是臺灣因有
僑務基礎、正體字和創新教學的大優勢，也能有自
己的一片天。（《臺灣光華雜誌》）

【解析】：此處表現了中英文語言習慣用法的不同，中文語言
習慣用法是從小到大，英文語言習慣用法是從大到
小。

例4

【原文】：**It is** in the interest of the parties concerned **that** the ne-
gotiations proceed at a relatively quick pace.

【譯文】：談判以相當快速的進度進行，都是以有關當事人的
利益出發。

【解析】：先翻譯強調句型的that子句。
英文強調句型：
It is/was 要強調部分（人、事、時、地、物）+ that
子句
搭配詞
adv. + rapid: exceptionally, extraordinarily, extremely,
unusually, very, fairly, quite, relatively

例5

【原文】：I think it interesting to go traveling.

= I think (that) it is interesting to go traveling.

【譯文】：我認為旅遊很有趣。

【解析】：think/believe/find/deem/consider 認為

interesting 很有趣 / worthwhile 很值得

I think it interesting to go traveling.

= I think (that) it is interesting to go traveling.

 例6

【原文】：It is not likely that you will be given a second opportunity.

【譯文】：人家不太可能再給你一次機會。

【解析】：it is likely 可能；it is not likely 不太可能

It is possible for him to come. 他可能會來。

= It is possible/likely/probable that he will come.

 例7

【原文】：How great a scientist she is!

What a great scientist she is!

【譯文】：她是個多麼偉大的科學家呀！

【解析】：驚嘆句型。

 例8

【原文】：他們結婚到現在已經十年了。

【譯文】：It has been ten years since they got married.

【解析】：先翻譯 "since" 自從。since 子句用過去式，主要句子用現在完成式。

第二章 中英翻譯的三個基本方法與轉換法的六個技巧

例9

【原文】：記得我的生日，你眞的很體貼。

【譯文】：It was really considerate of you to remember my birthday.

【解析】：先翻譯「你眞的很體貼」，然後翻譯「記得我的生日」。

例10

【原文】：他對大家都很體貼。

【譯文】：He was considerate of everyone.

【解析】：先翻譯「都很體貼」，然後翻譯「他對大家」。

例11

【原文】：It takes about one hour to go from Taichung to Taipei by HSR.

【譯文】：從臺中到臺北搭高鐵大約一小時。

【解析】：虛主詞 "It"。

HSR High Speed Rail 高鐵

例12

【原文】：It is unbelievable that she would win the lottery instead of me.

【譯文】：中樂透的是她而不是我，眞是不可思議。

【解析】：虛主詞 "It"。

例13

【原文】：It is very impolite to start eating before the host arrives.

【譯文】：主人還沒到就開始吃飯很失禮。

【解析】：虛主詞 "It"。

實用中英翻譯法

例14

【原文】：It is bad manners to interrupt.

【譯文】：打斷別人的話很不禮貌。

【解析】：虛主詞 "It"。先翻譯不定詞 "to interrupt"。

 例15

【原文】：A precipitous path leads down the cliff.

【譯文】：懸崖往下引入一條陡峭的山路。

【解析】：英文的 "leads down the cliff, a precipitous path" 與中文的位置重組。

 例16

【原文】：Houses in urban areas often have no individuality.

【譯文】：城市地區的房屋往往沒有一點特色。

【解析】：先翻譯 "in urban areas"。

 例17

【原文】：The Prime Minister is going to visit the United States next month.

【譯文】：首相下個月要出訪美國。

【解析】：先翻譯 "Prime Minister"，然後翻譯 "next month"，最後翻譯 "is going to visit the United States"。

 例18

【原文】：Canada's Prime Minister is the counterpart of the U.S. President.

【譯文】：加拿大總理相當於美國總統。

【解析】："counterpart" 翻譯「相當於」。

例19

【原文】：The UN imposed economic sanctions against Iraq.

【譯文】：聯合國對伊拉克實施經濟制裁。

【解析】：翻譯時，不需按照英文順序逐字翻譯，而需按照中文順序翻譯。

例20

【原文】：We have drafted a plan on the basis of recent research findings.

【譯文】：我們根據最近研究的發現擬定了一個計畫。

【解析】：先翻譯 "on the basis of" 「根據」，再翻譯「擬定了」。

work out, draw up, draft a plan 擬定

例21

【原文】：We had no difficulty in getting in touch with him.

【譯文】：我們和他取得聯繫沒有什麼困難。

【解析】：先翻譯「和他取得聯繫」再翻譯「沒有什麼困難」。

例22

【原文】：He laughed when he thought about the vicissitudes of this romance.

【譯文】：當他想起這段戀情的滄桑，他笑了。

【解析】：先翻譯副詞子句「當他想起這段感情的滄桑」。

vicissitudes [vəˋsɪsəˌtjudz] 變遷，世事變化

例23

【原文】：The export of the company this year has increased by 20 percent as compared with last year.

【譯文】：這家公司今年的出口與去年比較增加了20%。

【解析】：先翻譯「比去年」。

　　　　as compared with... = compared with... 與……比較

　　　　compare to... 將……比作

例24

【原文】：The psychiatrist explained her mental problem in home-ly terms.

【譯文】：那位精神科醫師用淺顯的詞語解釋了她的問題。

【解析】：先翻譯「那位精神科醫師」，再來翻譯「用淺顯的詞語」，最後翻譯「解釋了他的問題」。

　　　　psychiatrist [saɪˋkaɪətrɪst] 精神科醫師；精神病學家

例25

【原文】：The sales manager of the international trade department explained L/C terms to her assistant in plain Englilsh.

【譯文】：那位國貿部門的銷售經理用簡單明瞭的英語向她的助理解釋信用狀條款。

【解析】：先翻譯「那位國貿部門的銷售經理」，再來翻譯「用簡單明瞭的英語」，然後翻譯「向她的助理」，最後翻譯「解釋信用狀條款」。

　　　　in plain English 用淺顯的英語

　　　　Letter of Credit (L/C) 信用狀

（六）綜合技巧（Synthesizing Skill）

　　第六個技巧就是綜合技巧，綜合技巧就是掌握原文的涵義，根據譯文的文化思考模式、句法正確道地和慣用語法，來綜合運用翻譯的各種方法或技巧將原文翻譯成譯文。譯者翻譯時，不受限於原文的表面結構（surface structure），譯者靈活妥善運用翻譯的各種方法或技巧，使譯文句法正確，語意更明白流暢，以便忠實地傳達原文的意思

（「信」），充分地傳達原文的涵義（「達」），優雅地傳達原文的意境（「雅」）。

例1

【原文】：Someone's sitting in the shade today because someone planted a tree a long time ago. ── Warren Buffett

【譯文】：前人種樹，後人乘涼。── 華倫‧巴菲特

【解析】："someone" 譯成「前人、後人」，because 則減譯。

例2

【原文】：The two technological universities signed an agreement, under which they would exchange professors and students.

【譯文】：這兩所科技大學，簽定了協議，決定交換教授和學生。

【解析】：拆句：The two universities signed an agreement
減譯：under which they would

例3

【原文】：清水斷崖崖壁高度平均超過800公尺，行走崖上，生死懸於一線，稍有失足，便萬劫不復。（《臺灣光華雜誌》）

【譯文】：With the cliff rising to an average height of more than 800 meters, the journey along the road that runs across the cliff face is a precipitous one. (*Taiwan Panorama*)

【解析】：增譯：the journey
減譯：稍有失足
轉換：便萬劫不復
險峻的 precipitous

第三章 綜合練習

3-1 前　言（Preface）

　　許多學者主張：廣博閱讀（extensive reading）是增進學術能力的最佳途徑。同樣的，大量的練習也是增進翻譯造詣的不二法門。美國著名的溝通專家，著有 *Talk like TED* 的 Carmine Gallo 分析賈伯斯（Steve Jobs）上臺口頭報告成功有幾項因素，其中一個祕訣就是 "Rehearse, rehearse, and rehearse." 他每次上臺前一定會練習、練習再練習。翻譯是需要學習與練習的，許多專家、學者都持相同的看法。編者殷切期望以上所介紹的翻譯方法與技巧，能有助於提升學生的中英文翻譯品質與效率。學生若能藉由廣博翻譯（extensive translation）、密集翻譯（intensive translation）、專業翻譯（specific translation）循序漸進，配合學習與練習上述的翻譯方法與技巧，假以時日，就可以熟能生巧，提升翻譯與口譯的能力。

　　以下先熟悉英文長句的斷句、翻譯步驟與方法。

3-2 英文長句的斷句與翻譯（Making Pauses in and Translating a Long English Sentence）

　　雖然英翻中時看到後位修飾詞that, which, who或其他後位修飾詞（如：of, Ving, P.P.）會有些令人不知所措，但是這些that, which, who或其他後位修飾詞，在翻譯英文長句時恰好是很好的解析翻譯方法。雖然英文長句看起來較複雜，但是也有很多翻譯的方法與技巧可資運用。只要能夠掌握以下方法與步驟，就能順利翻譯英文長句：（1）了解大意；（2）知道如何斷句；（3）熟悉英文的基本句型結構，靈活運用各種中英翻譯方法與技巧；（4）確認譯文符合「信、達、雅」的標準。最後確認翻譯的作品是否符合譯文（translated language）的文化思考模式（cultural thought patterns）、句法正確道地（syntactic correctness and authenticity）、慣用語法（common expressions）。請看下面的英文句型圖表：

英文一般皆有主詞（Subject）＋動詞（Verb）的基本要素。大意一定是內容字（content words），如：主詞、動詞，受詞或補語，不會是功能字（function words），如：the/a/an或修飾語（adj.）、介詞片語、形容詞子句。

英文句型圖表：

The	Prep. Phrase (of the...)	
A + (Adj.) + N. **(S.)** + Adj. Clause (who/which + S. V.) + **V. (+ O./C.)**		
An	P.P. (-ed)	
	V+ing	

以下介紹翻譯英文長句的步驟和方法：

翻譯英文長句時，主要的步驟為：（1）了解大意；（2）斷句；（3）解析與翻譯；（4）確認譯文符合「信、達、雅」標準。

• 了解大意

將英文長句分成主要結構與次要結構。英文句子的主要結構是 S. + V. + O./C.。先了解英文句子的主要結構，即主詞＋動詞＋受詞或補語。遇到英文長句時，首先需從頭到尾完整地閱讀一遍，了解全句大意。即使閱讀過程中遇到不清楚的字詞時先別急著查單字。如果一開始就逐字解析翻譯文句，可能會平白花費精力與時間，無法掌握全句核心。

• 斷句

建議先了解整句大意後，再進行斷句。斷句時，將英文長句分成：（1）主要結構大單位（S. + V. + O./C.）；（2）次要結構小單位

（如：介系詞片語、形容詞子句、時間副詞、地方副詞、連接詞、子句等等）。

斷句的原則如下：

• 斷句原則：

1. 主詞／動詞／受詞（補語）每一個單位間停頓

2. 連接詞／對等連接詞之前停頓 and/or/but, either... or..., both... and..., neither... nor, not only... but also...

3. 修飾語／介系詞之前停頓（of the..., who/which/that, p.p., Ving）

4. 不定詞前停頓（to + V.）

5. 片語前後停頓（e.g., in order to, along with, as well as, tackle with...）

6. 平行結構前後停頓（e.g., through identifying, analyzing and re-sponding to potential risks）

• **解析與翻譯**

解析英文句子結構，翻譯時妥善運用中英翻譯方法與技巧。然後，按照英文句子結構語序排列，適切運用各種翻譯的方法（增加、減少、轉換）與技巧（改變、拆句、合併、肯定句否定句交換、重組、綜合），決定詞類（名詞、動詞、形容詞、副詞），語態（主、被動語態）或句型的轉換。英文句子裡的修飾成分常會出現介系詞片語、形容詞子句、現在分詞或過去分詞的後位修飾，此時可根據英文語序或常用表達方式來修改。例如："the long-running accusations filling German and Greek tabloids" 可翻為「德國和希臘小報上長期充滿的相互指控」。被動或主動語態的句子也可根據情況轉換。例如："the spendthrift Greeks should be taught to live by European rules" 可翻為「應該教導揮霍無度的希臘人遵守歐洲規定」。

• 確認譯文符合「信、達、雅」標準

　　翻譯完成後，重新閱讀原文和譯文，確認沒有遺漏，語序上的重組也沒有改變原句的意思，語意讀起來才會自然又清楚，確認譯文符合「信、達、雅」標準，如此翻譯即大功告成。

　　唯須注意，不同譯者使用的步驟或前後順序可能不太一樣。而斷句、語序、詞類、語態、句型的選擇上，也可能因人而異。然而，語言是很靈活的，一個句子可能有很多種翻譯方法，端視譯者中英文造詣，以及能否靈活運用上述翻譯方法與技巧，與能否將文意流暢貼切地傳達給讀者，並達成「信、達、雅」的要求與標準。最後確認譯文是否符合目標語或譯文的文化思考模式、句法正確道地及慣用語法，如此經常練習，翻譯英文長句時就能順利完成。

　　以下示範如何將英文長句翻譯成中文：

例1：請先全句從頭到尾閱讀一次。

Over the eight years from 2006 up to last year, 407 people in Yunlin County died in traffic accidents because they rode scooters without helmets or did not wear them properly, causing tragedies for countless broken families. (*Taipei Times*)

- 了解大意：閱讀此句時，需先找出主要結構與次要結構，即找出主要結構之主詞與動詞。

  主要結構：407 people in Yunlin County died in traffic accidents

  次要結構：because they rode scooters without helmets or did not wear
  　　　　　them properly

- 斷句：依照句法結構與句子中的字詞組合，將句子斷句成如下的小單元：

  Over the eight years/ from 2006 up/ to last year/, 407 people/ in Yunlin County/ died/ in traffic accidents/ because they rode scooters/ without

helmets/ or did not wear them/ properly/, causing tragedies/ for countless broken families.

- 解析英文句子結構，翻譯時妥善運用中英翻譯方法與技巧：

  （1）Over the eight years 8年來

  （2）from 2006 up 從2006年

  （3）to last year 到去年

  （4）407 people 407人

  （5）in Yunlin County 在雲林縣

  （6）died 死亡

  （7）in traffic accidents 在交通意外

  （8）because they rode scooters 因為他們騎機車

  （9）without helmets 沒有安全帽

  （10）or did not wear them 或沒戴安全帽

  （11）properly 正確地

  （12）causing tragedies 造成悲劇

  （13）for countless broken families 無數破碎家庭

  試著翻譯：從2006年到去年8年來，雲林縣407人因為他們騎機車沒
  有戴安全帽或沒正確地戴安全帽死於交通意外造成悲劇
  而使得無數家庭破碎。

- 確認譯文符合信、達、雅標準：

  從2006年至去年8年來，雲林縣共有407人因騎乘機車未戴或未正確
  配戴安全帽發生車禍死亡，造成無數家庭破碎悲劇。

例2：請先全句從頭到尾閱讀一次。

**Every department in the government should have a set of standard
operating procedures for responding to emergency situations.**

- 了解大意：閱讀此句時，需先找出主要結構與次要結構，即找出主

要結構之主詞與動詞。

主要結構：Every department should have

次要結構：in the government, for responding to emergency situations

- **斷句**：依照句法結構與句子中的字詞組合，將句子斷句成如下的小
單元：

Every department/ in the government/ should have/ a set of / standard
operating procedures/ for responding/ to emergency situations.

- **解析英文句子結構，翻譯時妥善運用中英翻譯方法與技巧：**
  - （1）Every department 每一個部門
  - （2）in the government 在政府中
  - （3）should have 應該有
  - （4）a set of 一套的
  - （5）standard operating procedures 標準的作業程序
  - （6）for responding 來反應
  - （7）to emergency situations 對緊急情況

  試著翻譯：在政府中，每一個部門，應該有一套的標準的作業程序
  　　　　　對緊急情況來反應。

- **確認譯文符合信、達、雅原則：**

  政府的各個部門都應該有一套標準作業流程來因應緊急情況。

例3：請先全句從頭到尾閱讀一次。

With the popularity of smartphones, checking Facebook, chatting, playing games and swiping a cellphone screen are common and totally normal occurrences, and more and more people are becoming heavy users. (*Taipei Times*)

- **了解大意**：閱讀此句時，需先找出主要結構與次要結構，即找出主
要結構之主詞與動詞。

主要結構：checking Facebook, chatting, playing games and swiping a cellphone screen are common and totally normal occurrences, more and more people are becoming heavy users

次要結構：with the popularity of smartphones

• **斷句**：依照句法結構與句子中的字詞組合，將句子斷句成如下的小單元：

With the popularity/ of smartphones/, checking Facebook/, chatting/, playing games/ and swiping a cellphone screen/ are common and totally normal occurrences/, and more and more people/ are becoming/ heavy users

• 解析英文句子結構，翻譯時妥善運用中英翻譯方法與技巧：

（1）With the popularity 隨著普及

（2）of smartphones 智慧型手機

（3）checking Facebook 看臉書

（4）chatting 聊天

（5）playing games 玩遊戲

（6）and swiping a cellphone screen 和滑手機

（7）are common 普遍

（8）and totally normal occurrences 和完全正常事情

（9）and more and more people 而愈來愈多人

（10）are becoming 正成為

（11）heavy users 重度使用者

試著翻譯：隨著智慧型手機普及，看臉書、聊天、玩遊戲和滑手機是很普遍而完全正常的事情，而愈來愈多人正成為重度使用者。

• **確認譯文符合信、達、雅標準：**

智慧型手機普及，看臉書、聊天、玩遊戲、滑手機，每天做這些事情再正常不過，更有人成為重度使用者。

例4：請先全句從頭到尾閱讀一次。

A sand sculpture portraying characters from the One Piece manga series is pictured at the Fulong International Sand Sculpture Art Festival in Keelung on May 4, 2013. (*Taipei Times*)

- 了解大意：閱讀此句時，需先找出主要結構與次要結構，即找出主要結構之主詞與動詞。

  主要結構：A sand sculpture is pictured at...in Keelung on May 4, 2013.

  次要結構：portraying characters from...

- 斷句：依照句法結構與句子中的字詞組合，將句子斷句成如下的小單元：

  A sand sculpture/ portraying characters/ from the One Piece manga series/ is pictured/ at the Fulong International Sand Sculpture Art Festival/ in Keelung/ on May 4/, 2013.

- 解析英文句子結構，翻譯時妥善運用中英翻譯方法與技巧：

  （1）A sand sculpture 一個沙雕

  （2）portraying characters 刻畫人物

  （3）from the One Piece manga series 從航海王的卡通

  （4）is pictured 被照相

  （5）at the Fulong International Sand Sculpture Art Festival 於福隆國際沙雕藝術季

  （6）in Keelung 在基隆

  （7）on May 4, 2013 在2013年5月4日

  試著翻譯：一個從航海王的卡通刻畫的沙雕人物，被照相在基隆於福隆國際沙雕藝術季在2013年5月4日。

- 確認譯文符合信、達、雅原則：

  藝術家於福隆國際沙雕藝術季刻畫出航海王的卡通人物。攝於2013年5月4日，基隆。

例5：請先全句從頭到尾閱讀一次。

At this point, the long-running accusations filling German and Greek tabloids－that the spendthrift Greeks should be taught to live by European rules; that the relentless austerity demanded by Germany and other lenders has served only to destroy Greece's economy and its ability to pay back its gargantuan debts－don't matter much. (*The New York Times*)

- 了解大意：閱讀此句時，需先找出主要結構與次要結構，即找出主要結構之主詞與動詞。

  主要結構：accusations don't matter much

  次要結構：－that the spendthrift Greeks should be taught to live by European rules; that the relentless austerity demanded by Germany and other lenders has served only to destroy Greece's economy and its ability to pay back its gargantuan debts－

- 斷句：

  At this point, / the long-running accusations / filling German and Greek tabloids－/ that the spendthrift Greeks / should be taught / to live / by European rules; /that the relentless austerity / demanded by Germany / and other lenders / has served / only to destroy Greece's economy / and its ability / to pay back/ its gargantuan debts－/ don't matter much.

- 解析英文句子結構，翻譯時妥善運用中英翻譯方法與技巧：

  （1）"At this point" 時間副詞，翻譯為「在這個節骨眼上」。

  （2）主詞為 "the long-running accusations"「長期的相互指控」，動詞為 "don't matter much"，英文主要句子結構為 "the long-running accusations don't matter much" 翻譯為「長期充滿的相互指控也不是那麼重要」。

（3）"filling German and Greek tabloids" 是形容詞子句；"which fill German and Greek tabloids" 翻譯為「德國和希臘小報上充滿的」。

（4）"that the spendthrift Greeks should be taught to live by European rules" 名詞子句被動語態 "should be taught" 轉譯為主動語態，翻譯為「應該教導揮霍無度的希臘人遵守歐洲規定」。

（5）"that the relentless austerity demanded by Germany and other lenders has served only to destroy Greece's economy and its ability to pay back its gargantuan debts" 為名詞子句，翻譯為「德國和其他債權人不斷要求的撙節政策只會破壞希臘的經濟和其償付龐大債務的能力」。

試著翻譯：在這個節骨眼上，德國和希臘小報上充滿的相互指控也不是那麼重要，應該教導揮霍無度的希臘人遵守歐洲規定，德國和其他債權人不斷要求的撙節政策只會破壞希臘的經濟和其償付龐大債務的能力。

• **確認譯文符合信、達、雅標準：**

在這個節骨眼上，德國和希臘小報上長期充滿的相互指控也不是那麼重要，這些相互指控包括：（1）應該教導揮霍無度的希臘人遵守歐洲規定；（2）德國和其他債權人不斷要求的撙節政策只會破壞希臘的經濟和其償付龐大債務的能力。

以下依序涵蓋句子練習、英文段落練習、英文文章練習、公職考試翻譯考題練習與教育部中英文翻譯能力檢定考試試題練習。

3-3 句子翻譯練習與解析（Practices and Analyses of Sentences Translation）

例1 ：（*BBC News*）（例1～例3）

【原文】：Scientists in Israel have discovered how ants cooperate to move big chunks of food back to their nests.

【譯文】：以色列的科學家們已經發現螞蟻是如何協力把大塊的食物搬回牠們的巢穴。

【解析】："Scientists in Israel" 翻譯成「以色列的科學家們」。

例2

【原文】：A large team of ants does the heavy lifting but they lack direction, while a small number of "scouts" intervene and steer for short periods.

【譯文】：一大隊的螞蟻搬運重物卻缺乏方向感，而少數的「偵查兵」介入其中並掌舵一小段時間。

【解析】："does the heavy lifting" 翻譯成「搬運重物」。"while" 翻譯成「而」。

例3

【原文】：They appear to have a mathematically perfect balance between individuality and conformism, the researchers said.

【譯文】：數名研究員表示，牠們似乎在個體和盲從因襲之間展現出數學式的完美平衡。

【解析】：先翻譯「數名研究員表示」。

individuality [ˌɪndəˌvɪdʒʊˋælətɪ] 個體；個體狀態

conformism [kənˋfɔrmɪzm̩] 盲從因襲的態度

例4：（*BBC News*）（例4～例11）

【原文】：South Korea declares "de facto end" to MERS virus.

【譯文】：南韓宣布事實上結束MERS疫情。

【解析】：de facto end 事實上結束

例5

【原文】：The prime minister apologised for the government's response to the outbreak.

【譯文】：針對政府面對疫情爆發的回應，總理表示歉意。

【解析】：先翻譯 "the government's response to the outbreak"。

outbreak [ˋaʊtˌbrek] 爆發

例6

【原文】：South Korea's Prime Minister Hwang Kyo-ahn has declared a "de facto end" to the outbreak of the Middle East Respiratory Virus (MERS).

【譯文】：南韓總理黃教安已宣布事實上已結束中東呼吸症候群（MERS）的疫情。

【解析】：de facto [dɪˋfækto]【法】事實上（的）

例7

【原文】：Mr. Hwang said that as there had been no new infections for 23 days, the public "can now be free from worry".

【譯文】：黃總理表示已經有23天未出現新的感染，「民眾現在可以不用擔心」。

【解析】：be free from 免於；無……之憂

例8

【原文】：He also apologised for the government's much-criticised response to the virus, which has killed 36 people in South Korea, Yonhap news agency reports.

【譯文】：政府對病毒疫情作出的回應飽受批評，對此他也表示歉意。該病毒已在南韓奪走36條人命。南韓聯合通訊社報導。

【解析】：也可以先翻譯「南韓聯合通訊社報導」，政府對病毒疫情作出的回應飽受批評，對此他也表示歉意。該病毒已在南韓奪走36條人命。

 例9

【原文】：But the WHO said it was not yet declaring MERS officially over.

【譯文】：然而世界衛生組織（ＷＨＯ）表示尚未正式宣布MERS疫情解除。

【解析】：World Health Organization (WHO) 世界衛生組織

 例10

【原文】：A spokeswoman in Manila said the World Health Organisation required 28 days without a new infection to make the announcement－twice the incubation period of the virus. The last case was confirmed in South Korea on 4 July.

【譯文】：馬尼拉的一位女發言人表示，世界衛生組織需要28天，亦即病毒潛伏期的兩倍時間，都沒有出現新的傳染，世界衛生組織才能宣布疫情解除。南韓最後一個確診病例是在7月4日。

【解析】：incubation [ˌɪnkjəˈbeʃən] 【醫】潛伏期

confirm [kənˈfɝm] 證實；確定

例11

【原文】：South Korean Health Ministry official Kwon Duk-cheol said precautions, including screening at airports, would remain in place "until the situation comes to a formal end", AFP news agency reports.

"We still have many arrivals from the Middle East so there is always a possibility that new patients can come in," he added.

【譯文】：法新社報導：大韓民國保健部官員Kwon Duk-cheol 表示，會保持包括機場檢查在內的預防措施準備就緒，「直到疫情正式解除」。

他補充說道：「我們依然有許多從中東抵達的人們，因此總是有可能會有新的病患進來」。

【解析】：in place 在正確位置；準備妥當；準備就緒

possibility [ˌpɑsəˈbɪlətɪ] 可能性

There is a good possibility of rain tonight. 今晚很可能會下雨。

例12 ：（*BBC News*）（例12～例20）

【原文】：Facebook is now used by half of world's online users.

【譯文】：現在世界有半數的網路使用者使用臉書。

例13

【原文】：Half the world's estimated online population now check into social networking giant Facebook at least once a month.

【譯文】：現在世界估計的上網人口（網路使用人口）中，有一半的人至少每個月看一次（點閱一次）社群網路巨人——臉書。

【解析】：check into 到達並在……登記

She has just checked into the hotel. 她剛剛在旅館辦好住宿登記。

例14

【原文】：Facebook said the number of people who check into the social network at least monthly grew 13% to 1.49 billion in the three months to the end of June.

【譯文】：臉書表示，在截至6月底的過去3個月裡，使用臉書的人數至少每個月增加13%，目前已達14億9千萬人。

【解析】：billion [ˋbɪljən] 10億

例15

【原文】：The number is equal to half of the estimated three billion people who use the internet worldwide.

【譯文】：這個人數等於世界預估的30億網路使用人口的一半。

【解析】：equal [ˋikwəl] 相等的；相當的；均等的

A dime is equal to 10 cents. 一角的硬幣相當於10美分。

例16

【原文】：Of those users, it said well over half, 65%, were now accessing Facebook daily.

【譯文】：在那些使用者中，有超過一半，也就是65%的人，現在每天使用臉書。

【解析】：access 使用

例17

【原文】：The rise in monthly active users helped drive second quarter revenue up 39% year-on-year to \$4.04bn (£2.6bn).

【譯文】：因為每個月活躍使用者增加，促使第2季收益比去年同期增加39%至40億4千萬美元（26億英鎊）。

【解析】：增譯「因為」。

year-on-year 與上年同期數字相比較

drive 驅動

revenue [ˈrɛvəˌnju] 各項收入，總收入

例18

【原文】：Mobile advertising revenue was the biggest factor, accounting for more than three quarters of the total.

【譯文】：手機廣告收益是最大的因素，占超過總收益的 $\frac{3}{4}$。

【解析】：mobile advertising 汽車廣告或手機廣告，看前後文決定

account for（在數量等上）占

例19

【原文】：In the US, the company said people were now spending more than one out of every five minutes on their smartphones on Facebook.

【譯文】：臉書公司表示，在美國，人們現在每5分鐘就有超過一分鐘是透過智慧型手機使用臉書。

【解析】：（1）spend...on... 花（錢），花費

He spent US\$100 on the bike.

他花了100美元買下那輛自行車。

（2）spend...Ving... 花（時間，精力）

They spent three months traveling Europe.

他們花了3個月時間遊覽歐洲。

【原文】：Meanwhile, speculation is continuing over when President Ma Ying-jeou will visit Taiping Island, one of the disputed South China Sea islands that is under de facto Taiwanese control. In June, Ma said that he may visit the island before the end of his term.

【譯文】：同時，馬英九總統還在思索何時造訪太平島，該島是具爭議的南海群島中的其中一島，該島在臺灣實際統治之下。6月時，馬總統表示他可能會在其任期結束前造訪該島。

【解析】：de facto 【法】事實上（的）

例21 ：（*Pakistan Defence* 2015-07-28）（例21～例22）

【原文】：KMT lawmakers threaten reprisal over Lee's Diaoyoutai comment.

【譯文】：針對李登輝總統的釣魚臺評論，國民黨立法委員威脅將報復。

【原文】：A politician on Monday accused former President Lee Teng-hui of treason for his recent remarks on the Diaoyutai Islands, as ruling Kuomintang (KMT) lawmakers threatened to revoke Lec's privileges as a former head of state.

第三章

綜合練習

例20

例22

【譯文】：由於前總統李登輝針對釣魚臺群島做出的評論，一位政治人物於週一指控李前總統犯下叛國罪，同時執政的國民黨立法委員威脅將要撤銷李前總統所享受的特權。

【解析】：accuse sb. of sth. 控告
treason 叛國罪
lawmaker, legislator 立法委員

例23：（*CNA* 2015-08-02）（例23～例29）

【原文】：Chinese coast guard vessels patrol Diaoyutai waters.

【譯文】：中國籍海巡船巡邏釣魚臺水域。

【解析】：coast guard 海上防衛隊
vessels 船艦

例24

【原文】：A flotilla of three Chinese coast guard vessels patrolled waters near the disputed Diaoyutai Islands in the East China Sea Sunday, according to a statement posted on the Website of China's State Oceanic Administration.

【譯文】：根據中國國家海洋局發表的一則聲明，3艘中國籍海巡船所組成的小型艦隊於週日巡邏靠近位於東海具爭議的釣魚臺群島。

【解析】：flotilla [floˋtɪlə] 小型艦隊
according to 根據
China's State Oceanic Administration 中國國家海洋局

例25

【原文】：This is the 22nd time that Chinese vessels have patrolled the waters 12 miles within the island group this year, the administration said. The last time that Chinese vessels sailed into the disputed waters was on July 29.

【譯文】：海洋局表示，這是中國艦隊今年第22次於距離群島12海里內的水域巡邏。艦隊上一次是於7月29日駛入具爭議的水域。

【解析】：patrol 巡邏

sail 航行

例26

【原文】：Chinese vessels patrolled the Diaoyutai waters 35 times in 2014 and 50 times in 2013, respectively, according to China News Service, quoting official records.

【譯文】：根據中國新聞社引述的官方紀錄，中國籍艦隊在釣魚臺水域巡邏分別是2014年35次和2013年50次。

【解析】：vessels 艦隊

例27

【原文】：The Diaoyutais, some 100 nautical miles northeast of Taiwan, are also claimed by Taiwan and China, which calls them the Diaoyu Islands.

【譯文】：臺灣和大陸皆主張位於臺灣東北方約100海里的釣魚臺為其所有，並稱之為釣魚臺群島。

【解析】：nautical [`nɔtɪk!] 海上的；航海的

例28

【原文】：The Diaoyutai Islands, as they are known in Taiwan, have been under Japan's administrative control since 1972, and are called the Senkaku Islands in Japan.

【譯文】：臺灣所認知的釣魚臺群島，自1972年以來歸於日本的行政統治之下，而且日本稱之爲尖閣諸島。

例29

【原文】：Yemen is in the grip of its most severe crisis in years, as competing forces fight for control of the country.

【譯文】：因爲數個競爭勢力爲了奪取國家的控制權而爭鬥，所以多年來葉門陷入最嚴重的危機。

【解析】：本句翻譯運用到重組技巧，先翻「因爲」，然後翻「所以」。

grip 掌握；控制

in years 多年來

as 因爲

例30 ：（*BBC News*）（例30～例31）

【原文】：Impoverished but strategically important, the tussle for power in Yemen has serious implications for the region and the security of the West.

【譯文】：葉門雖然貧困但具戰略重要性，葉門的權力鬥爭對於區域和西方安全有重要含意（意涵）。

【解析】：tussle 爭鬥

implications 含意；意涵

例31

【原文】：The main fight is between forces loyal to the beleaguered President, Abdrabbuh Mansour Hadi, and those allied to Zaidi Shia rebels known as Houthis, who forced Mr Hadi to flee the capital Sanaa in February.

【譯文】：主要的爭鬥是在於效忠被圍困的哈迪總統的這一派，以及那些與被稱爲青年運動的扎伊迪什葉派同

盟的反叛軍之間。而青年運動於2月迫使哈迪總統逃
離首都沙那。

【解析】：Abdrabbuh Mansour Hadi 哈迪

Shia 什葉派

Houthis 青年運動（支持胡塞武裝組織）

3-4 段落翻譯練習與解析（Practices and Analyses of Paragraphs Translation）

例1

【原文】：希臘國會通過撙節方案《華爾街日報》

希臘國會16日清晨通過換取新紓困金所需的撙節方
案，國會300席中有229名議員投下同意票，擁有149
席的執政黨「激進左翼聯盟」中則有32人投下反對
票、6人棄權及1人缺席。

【譯文】：**Greece's Parliament Passes Austerity Measures Required for Bailout** (*The Wall Street Journal*)

Greece Parliament passed austerity measures required to secure a fresh bailout on 16th at dawn. Of the 300 seats in the Parliament, 229 agreed. And among the 149 seats of the ruling left-wing Syriza party in the Parliament, 32 voted against them, 6 abstained in the election, and 1 absented himself/herself.

【解析】：parliament [ˋpɑrləmənt] 議會；國會

換取 secure

新紓困金 fresh bailout

撙節方案 austerity measures

在……之中；在……中間 of the...; among the...

席 seat

激進左翼聯盟 left-wing Syriza party

棄權 abstain

例2

【原文】：**Deal Reached on Iran Nuclear Program (*The New York Times* 2015/7/14)**

Iran and a group of six nations led by the United States reached a historic accord on Tuesday to significantly limit Tehran's nuclear ability for more than a decade in return for lifting international oil and financial sanctions.

【譯文】：6強與伊朗達成核武協議（《紐約時報》2015年7月14日）

伊朗與以美國爲首的6國集團週二宣布達成歷史性協議。伊朗政府未來10多年的核武能力將受到大幅限制，以交換西方國家解除對伊朗石油和金融的國際制裁。

【解析】：reach a historic accord 達成歷史性協議

to reach/come to/an agreement/accord/terms 達成協議

nuclear ability 核武能力

in return for 交換；作爲回報

lift, remove, disencumber; dissolve; divest; relieve 解除

sanction; impose sanctions against 制裁

例3

【原文】：伊朗與六強簽署核協議（《衛報》）

伊朗已和美、英、法、德、俄及中國大陸在維也納達成核子協議，伊朗的核子計畫將面臨長期的嚴格限制，而國際社會將逐步解除對伊朗的制裁。美國總統歐巴馬表示，這份協議是阻止伊朗取得核武的最佳可行選項。

【譯文】：**Iran nuclear deal: world powers reach historic agreement to lift sanctions (*The Guardian*)**

Iran and the U.S, the U.K., France, Germany, Russia, and China have concluded the nuclear deal in Vienna. Long-term severe limitations will be imposed on Iran's nuclear program, while international societies will progressively lift sanctions on Iran. American President Barack Obama said that the agreement was the best option available to prevent Iran from acquiring nuclear weapons.

【解析】：（1）達成協議 to reach an agreement; to come to an agreement; to come to terms; to make a bargain; to settle a bargain; to conclude a bargain

（2）限制 to impose/place limitations on

（3）當president後面緊接一國總統的名字時要大寫，但其後若未緊接名字，只是指總統，則不大寫。例如：

U.S. President Barack Obama cannot run for his third term.（美國總統歐巴馬不能競選第三任。）

（4）available 放在名詞後面

例4

【原文】：伊拉克盼核協議有助美國及伊朗兩大盟邦關係（《華盛頓郵報》）

儘管許多中東國家目前仍對伊朗核協議感到懷疑，伊拉克當局卻表示歡迎，並期盼該協議能緩和美國及伊朗間緊張關係，以重振打擊「伊斯蘭國」好戰分子之力量。

【譯文】：**Iraq hopes U.S.-Iran nuclear accord will put an end to its divided loyalties (*Washington Post*)**

In spite of the fact that many Middle East countries have been suspicious of the Iran nuclear deal so far, Iraqi authorities embrace it, hoping it will ease the tension between the United States and Iran in order to reinvigorate the power against militants of Islamic State.

【解析】：（1）轉譯：

伊拉克盼核協議有助美國及伊朗兩大盟邦關係。

Iraq hopes U.S.-Iran nuclear accord will put an end to its divided loyalties.

（2）In spite of the fact that = Despite the fact that

（3）感到懷疑 be suspicious of

（4）緩和緊張關係 ease the tension

（5）重振 reinvigorate

（6）伊斯蘭國 Islamic State

例5

【原文】：During the Cold War, U.S. officials viewed Africa strictly through the lens of Soviet competition. In the 1990s, scarred by "Black Hawk Down" in Somalia and our impotence to stop the genocide in Rwanda, Africa didn't so much as fall off Washington's radar as it was deliberately erased. By the end of his administration, however, President Bill Clinton recognized Africa was becoming more strategic and pushed for a landmark trade bill, which was recently extended for another 10 years. (CNN)

【譯文】：在冷戰期間，美國官員嚴格地通過與蘇聯競爭的視角來看非洲。在1990年代，索馬利亞「黑鷹計畫」所留下來的創傷，以及我們無力阻止盧安達的種族屠殺，使得非洲並未如我們蓄意想要消除地脫離華盛頓的雷達。然而，在柯林頓總統任期的結尾，他認清非洲正變得愈來愈有策略而推動重大貿易法案，而這個法案最近延長另一個十年。（CNN）

【解析】：impotence [`ɪmpətəns] 無能，無力

genocide [`dʒɛnəˌsaɪd] 種族滅絕；集體屠殺

not so much as...as... 不如……一樣……

fall off 脫離

deliberately [dɪ`lɪbərɪtlɪ] 故意地，蓄意地

erase [ɪ`res] 消除；清除

landmark [`lændˌmɑrk] （歷史上劃時代的）重大事件；里程碑

 例6 ：（*The New York Times*）（例6～例13）

【原文】：**Greece's Future, and the Euro's**

The referendum called by Greece's prime minister is a bad idea, but at this stage it's about the best available. Greek banks have been shut down to avoid a meltdown; bailout talks with European creditors are frozen; Athens does not have the money to pay 1.6 billion euros due to the International Monetary Fund on Tuesday, threatening default and withdrawal from the euro.

【譯文】：希臘和歐元的未來

希臘總理要求進行公民投票乃是個下策，但在現階段恐怕是可行的最佳方案。希臘的銀行已經關閉以免破產；與歐洲債權人之間的緊急財政援助談判凍結了。雅典沒有錢支付國際貨幣基金組織週四到期的16億歐元，揚言將違約並脫離歐元區。

【解析】：referendum [ˌrɛfəˋrɛndəm] 公民投票

meltdown [ˋmɛltˌdaʊn] 溶化；溶解。轉譯為「破產」。

bailout [ˋbelˌaʊt] 緊急（財政）援助

default [dɪˋfɔlt] 未履行債務；不履行；違約；拖欠

withdrawal [wɪðˋdrɔəl] 收回；撤回；撤清；撤退

 例7

【原文】：So, confronted with conditions from the lenders that he dismissed as "insulting," Prime Minister Alexis Tsipras made the surprise announcement on Saturday that he was putting the matter before Greek voters in a referendum to be held July 5.

【譯文】：希臘總理阿列克西斯·齊普拉斯將這個因債權人而來的情勢視為「侮辱」，並在面對該情事時，於週六發布驚人的公告，表示他將在7月5日舉行公投時，在希臘選民面前把這個問題提出來。

【解析】：confront [kənˋfrʌnt] with 使面對；使遇到

dismiss [dɪsˋmɪs] ...as... 把……當作……而不再去想

 例8

【原文】：Putting so complex and fateful a question on such short notice to a nation already so confused and battered is fraught with danger. But given the huge consequences of what is about to happen, the Greeks deserve a chance to say whether they want to stay in the euro, with all the continuing sacrifice that entails, or whether they are prepared for the near-term calamity and long-term unknowns of opting out. At the very least, Greece's creditors should extend their payment deadlines long enough to hear what the Greek voters say.

【譯文】：在這麼短的時間將如此複雜又重大的問題交付給一個已經如此困惑又憔悴的國家，乃是個充滿危險的舉動。然而考慮到將會發生哪些重大事情結果的情況下，希臘人應當有機會決定他們是否想要留在歐元區並承擔全部持續犧牲的責任，抑或他們預備好要面對退出歐元區後近期的災難和長期未知的事項。無論如何，希臘的債權人應當足夠地延長他們的付款期限以聽見希臘選民的聲音。

【解析】：notice [ˋnotɪs] 公告；通知

on such short notice 在如此短的時間

confuse [kənˋfjuz] 使困惑；使混亂

batter [ˋbætɚ] 衝擊

is fraught [frɔt] with 充滿……的；伴隨……的

given + prep. 介系詞；Given + N. 名詞 如果有；假如；考慮到

entail 必須；承擔

calamity [kəˋlæmətɪ] 災難

opt out 退出；不參加

例9

【原文】：The referendum question, released on Monday, will be perplexing to voters, but it doesn't really matter. The details of the demands over which the talks have collapsed, mostly dealing with pensions and value-added taxes, are not what the endgame is about. At this point, the long-running accusations filling German and Greek tabloids—Greeks should be taught to live by European rules; that the relentless austerity demanded by Germany and other lenders has served only to destroy Greece's economy and its ability to pay back its gargantuan debts—don't matter much.

【譯文】：星期一發布的公投問題將讓投票人感到困惑，但這無關緊要。在破局的談判中所提出的要求細節，其中大多跟退休金和加值稅有關，但這並非殘局關心之議題。在這個節骨眼上，德國和希臘小報上長期充滿的互相指控也不是那麼重要，這些互相指控包括：應該教導揮霍無度的希臘人遵守歐洲規定；德國和其他債權人不斷要求的撙節政策只會破壞希臘的經濟和其償付龐大債務的能力。

【解析】：release [rɪˋlis] 發布（新聞稿）

perplexing [pɚˋplɛksɪŋ] 困惑；複雜化

collapse [kəˋlæps]（計畫等）突然失敗

pension [ˋpɛnʃən] 退休金

endgame [ˋɛndˌgem] 殘局

accusation [ˌækjəˋzeʃən] 指控；控告；指責

tabloid [ˋtæblɔɪd]（以轟動性報導為特點的）小報

spendthrift [ˋspɛndˌθrɪft] 揮霍無度的人；揮霍無度的

relentless [rɪˋlɛntlɪs] 不間斷的；持續的

austerity [ɔˋstɛrətɪ] 緊縮、嚴格的節制消費

gargantuan [gɑrˋgæntʃuən] 龐大的；巨大的

【原文】：The question before the Greeks is whether they are prepared to abandon the euro. That is also the question that
Chancellor Angela Merkel of Germany, President Fran-
çois Hollande of France, Christine Lagarde, the managing director of the I.M.F., and other members of the eurozone must decide.

【譯文】：希臘人面臨的問題在於他們是否預備好要放棄歐
元。這也是德國總理安格拉・梅克爾、法國總統法
蘭索瓦・歐蘭德、國際貨幣基金組織總裁克莉絲蒂
娜・拉加德和歐元區其他成員國所必須決定的。

【解析】：Chancellor [ˋtʃænsələ] （德、奧等的）總理

managing director 常務董事

I.M.F. International Monetary Fund 國際貨幣基金組織

【原文】：The answer should be a resounding commitment to keep
Greece in the euro. Ms. Merkel on Monday revived a
phrase not heard in many months: "If the euro fails, Europe fails." A "Grexit" would seriously undermine the
credibility of the euro currency, threatening a global contagion. For Greece, an exit could mean losing the ability
to borrow from foreign investors, the potential collapse
of its banking system and a wave of litigation from cred-

itors and suppliers. President Obama has called both Ms. Merkel and Mr. Hollande to make clear American concerns about the effect it would have on global finance.

【譯文】：這個答案必須是徹底承諾讓希臘留在歐元區。梅克爾週一回憶起數月中未曾聽到的措辭：「如果歐元失敗，歐洲也會失敗。」「希臘退出」將會嚴重地逐漸損害歐元貨幣的信用，威脅恐蔓延全球。對希臘而言，退出可能意謂失去向國外投資人借款的能力，銀行體系潛在崩盤的可能性，以及興起和債權人與供應商之間訴訟的浪潮。歐巴馬總統已經致電梅克爾和歐蘭德，對於希臘退出歐元區將會對全球金融造成的影響，清楚地表達美國的關切。

【解析】：resounding [rɪˋzaʊndɪŋ] 響亮的；徹底的
commitment [kəˋmɪtmənt] 承諾；保證
undermine [ˌʌndɚˋmaɪn] 逐漸損害
credibility [ˌkrɛdəˋbɪlətɪ] 可信性；確實性
contagion [kənˋtedʒən]（情緒、思想等的）感染；感染性的情緒（或思想等）
litigation [ˌlɪtəˋgeʃən] 訴訟
creditor [ˋkrɛdɪtɚ] 債權人
debtor [ˋdɛtɚ] 債務人

例12

【原文】：But even if the Greeks vote to stay with the euro, the crisis will not be over. Under the policies currently demanded by the eurozone leaders, the Greeks will find their suffering worse and their prospects unchanged, and Mr. Tsipras may well be compelled to call for new national elections.

【譯文】：即使希臘人投票贊成留在歐元區，這個危機也還未
　　　　　結束。在歐元區領導者近來要求的政策之下，希臘
　　　　　人將發現其痛苦加劇以及他們的前景並沒有改變，
　　　　　然後齊普拉斯有可能會被迫舉行新的國家選舉。

【解析】：prospects [`prɑspɛkt] 前景；前途
　　　　　compel [kəm`pɛl] 強迫
　　　　　call for 要求；需要

 例13

【原文】　：The power to make things better ultimately lies with the
　　　　　eurozone and the I.M.F.. They have already started an
　　　　　unofficial campaign to influence Greek voters to stay
　　　　　with the euro by making public their terms for maintain-
　　　　　ing the bailout. They would make a far stronger case
　　　　　if they also vowed to do the one thing that would give
　　　　　Greeks a real incentive to stay and to initiate real re-
　　　　　forms. That is to start ripping up their i.o.u.s..

【譯文】：最終能讓事情好轉的權力取決於歐元區和國際貨幣
　　　　　基金組織的決定。他們已經展開一個非官方的活
　　　　　動，藉由公開他們維持緊急財政援助的條款，以促
　　　　　使希臘選民留在歐元區。他們會更加有理由，是否
　　　　　他們也發誓做一件會真正鼓勵希臘留下來並著手進
　　　　　行真正改革的事情，也就是開始撕毀他們的借據。

【解析】　：ultimately [`ʌltəmɪtlɪ] 最後；最終
　　　　　lie with 取決於……的決定
　　　　　campaign [kæm`pen] 運動；活動
　　　　　make a far stronger case 更加有理由

make a case（意謂give a reason）提出對某事有利的論據

incentive [ɪnˋsɛntɪv] 刺激；鼓勵；動機

initiate [ɪˋnɪʃɪˏet] 開始；創始；開始實施

rip up 把……撕成碎片

i.o.u.s. [ˋaɪˏoˋjuz] 借條

3-5 公職考試翻譯考題練習與解析

103年公務人員特種考試外交領事人員及外交行政人員

一、英譯中：請將下列英文譯為中文。

【原文】：The Gulf nation of Qatar is home to exiled Hamas leader Khaled Mashaal and is a key financial patron for the Gaza Strip, which Hamas controls. The Gulf state denies financially backing Hamas, however, and has sought to play a role in brokering a truce to end fighting between the Islamic State extremist group and Israel.

【譯文1】：遭到流放的哈馬斯組織（Hamas）領袖Khaled Mashaal正藏身在波斯灣小國卡達（Qatar），加薩走廊（Gaza Strip）是哈馬斯組織的地盤，其主要的資金來源正是Khaled Mashaal所提供。但是卡達卻否認金援哈馬斯組織一事，並積極居中斡旋爭取停火協議，以調解伊斯蘭國極端分子和以色列之間的衝突。

【解析】：（1）轉譯

control 動詞轉換成名詞「地盤」。

is home to 轉換成動詞「藏身在」。

（2）增譯："and is a key financial parton for the Gaza Strip" 其主要的資金來源正是 Khaled Mashaal 所提供。增譯「所提供」。

（3）be home to 是……的所在地

（4）exile [ˋɛksaɪl] 流放；流亡；離開本國；離鄉背井

（5）patron [ˋpetrən] 贊助者，資助者

（6）play a role in 扮演一角

（7）broker 以中間人等身分安排

（8）truce [trus] 停戰；休戰

【譯文2】：哈馬斯流亡領導人哈立德馬沙爾現居海灣國家卡達，而處於哈馬斯控制之下加薩走廊背後，該國也是最主要財政資助人。儘管該國否認在背後給予哈馬斯經濟援助，但在伊斯蘭國極端組織和以色列締結停火合約這一問題上，它想要扮演重要角色。

【解析】：改譯，將"The Gulf nation of Qatar is home to..."變成以人為主詞的「哈馬斯流亡領導人哈立德馬沙爾現居……」。按照中文習慣，將 "however"變成「雖然……但……」的結構。

二、中譯英：請將下列中文譯為英文。

題目1

【原文】：人們有時可能會把食物所引起的疾病誤認為流行性感冒，有些造成疾病的毒素毒性強到微小到如一粒鹽的份量可以在一小時內讓數人致死。

【譯文1】：Sometimes, the illness arising from food could be mistakenly viewed as influenza. Some toxins which cause diseases, even in a small dose like a grain of salt, could be disturbingly lethal to people within an hour.

【解析】：（1）轉譯：中文第一句是主動句，英文翻成被動句。

人們有時可能會把食物所引起的疾病誤認為流行性感冒。

Sometimes, the illness arising from food could be mistakenly viewed as influenza.

（2）增譯： "be disturbingly lethal" 中的 "disturbingly"

（3）【醫】流行性感冒 influenza [ˌɪnfluˋɛnzə]

（4）致命的 lethal [ˋliθəl]

（5）引起 to give rise to, to bring about, to arise from, to cause, to lead to

【譯文2】：People may sometimes mistakenly regard diseases caused by food as influenza, **but** some pathogens are **so toxic that** even a small dose such as a salt crystal can kill a person within one hour.

【解析】：（1）改譯，把原文「毒性強到」改成 "so toxic that...", 增譯連接詞but。

（2）主動：regard...as...v.t., take...as, think of...as, look on/upon...as, see...as, view...as, 把……看作，把……認為

（3）被動：be regarded as, be taken as, be thought of as, be looked on/upon as, be seen as, be viewed as

題目2

【原文】：大腦研究的發現證明了延遲獲得滿足感的人在有壓力時比較不會崩潰、僵住，甚或行為退化，他們勇於迎接挑戰，甚至在面臨困難時，他們非但沒有放棄，還追求挑戰。

【譯文1】：The findings of cerebral research indicate that there is comparatively less possibility of mental breakdown, emotional stiffness, and behavioral degeneration which may happen to those people when they are faced with pressure, who delayed

實用中英翻譯法

the acquisition of satisfaction. Yet, they bravely take challenges and barely give themselves up even in the face of difficulties. Instead, they always welcome any challenges with open arms.

【解析】：（1）轉換：主詞由人轉物 there is less possibility of...to those people..., who...。

（2）增譯：Instead, they always welcome any challenges with open arms.

（3）there is possibility/likelihood/probability 有可能

（4）獲得 to obtain, to acquire, to attain, to gain

（5）……的人 those/people/he/one who

God helps those who help themselves.

【諺】天助自助者（或：自助而後天助）。

（6）in the face of 面對

（7）with open arms 熱烈地；熱情地

【譯文2】：Studies about brains indicate that comparatively speaking, **those who postpone satisfaction attainment** are not likely to collapse, petrify, and even act backwardly in the face of pressure. Rather, they are warriors in front of challenges. Therefore, even when they are confronted with difficulty, they prefer to challenge it, rather than give it up.

【解析】：（1）順序改譯，將原文「延遲獲得滿足感的人」，改成形容詞子句 "those who postpone satisfaction attainment"。

（2）are not likely to, are unlikely to 不可能；不會

（3）comparatively, relatively, rather 比較

（4）in front of 在某人／某物前面

（5）prefer to 寧可，寧願（選擇）；更喜歡

（6）rather than 而不是……

103年公務人員高等考試一級暨二級考試試題

一、英譯中

【原文】：As is often the case in Ebola outbreaks, no one knows how the first person got the disease or how the virus found its way to the region. Some previous epidemics are thought to have begun when someone was exposed to blood while killing or butchering an infected animal. Cooking will destroy the virus, so the risk is not in eating the meat, but in handling it raw. People might also become infected by eating fruit or other un-cooked foods contaminated by droppings from infected bats.

【譯文1】：一如往常的當伊波拉病毒爆發之時，沒有人能夠知道第一個患病的病人是如何得病的，或該病毒是如何蔓延至該區域的。若干以前的傳染病被認為是透過血液傳染，係因屠宰、捕殺那些染病的動物。烹調會殺死該病毒，所以我們面臨的危機不是吃肉，而是未煮過時如何處理。人們也有可能因為食用受感染蝙蝠糞便污染的水果或其他生食而染病。

【解析】：（1）As is often the case 情況常常如此；這是常有的情形
　　　　　（2）轉譯：when someone was exposed to blood 透過血液傳染
　　　　　（3）增譯：the risk 我們面臨的危機
　　　　　（4）droppings [ˋdrɑpɪŋz] 鳥獸的糞便

【譯文2】：伊波拉疫情全面引爆，常見問題再次浮現。誰是首位感染者？病毒如何入侵疫區？人們認為先前血液為感染途徑，如宰殺受感染的動物。烹調可以殺死細菌，因此問題不是在攝食肉類，而是在處理生肉的過程。攝食水果或是被帶原蝙蝠的糞便所汙染的生食，都有可能使人感染。

【解析】：（1）增譯：outbreaks 全面引爆再次浮現

　　　　　（2）詞性轉換：but in handling it raw 而是在處理生肉的過程

　　　　　（3）重組：People might also become infected by eating fruit or other uncooked foods contaminated by droppings from infected bats. 攝食水果或是被帶原蝙蝠的糞便所汙染的生食，都有可能使人感染。

【譯文3】：此次伊波拉病毒爆發跟之前的情況是一樣的，沒人知道零號病人是怎麼染上病毒的，而病毒又是如何在該區蔓延。早期傳染病的起因可能是，人們在宰殺的過程中接觸到已受感染牲畜的血液。烹煮可以殺滅病毒，所以問題不在於吃肉，而是處理生肉的方式。吃受到蝙蝠汙染的水果或其他生食也可能受到感染。

【解析】：（1）"killing or butchering" 減譯成「宰殺」。

　　　　　（2）"risk" 轉譯成「問題」。

　　　　　（3）將 "People" 省譯。

二、中譯英

【原文】：如果你有金錢方面的問題，有很多不同的方式可以省錢。與其花錢買新衣服，試著到慈善商店買二手貨，在那裡你會發現很多時尚的廉價品。外食亦是一筆很大開銷，你可以跟幾個朋友一起煮食，既便宜又好玩。巴士與計程車也會讓你破費，所以值得買一輛便宜的腳踏車代步。

【譯文1】：If you are in financial difficulties, there are many ways to save your money. **Firstly**, rather than purchasing new clothes, you may try to purchase second-hand clothes in charity shops, where you may find many fashionable low-priced items. **Secondly**, eating out is very expensive. You may cook with some of your friends, which is cheap and interesting. **Finally**, taking the bus and taxi will incur the loss of your money. Therefore, it is worthwhile to buy a bicycle as a means of transportation.

【解析】：（1）增譯連接詞 firstly, secondly, finally 使文意通順。

（2）轉譯：如果你有金錢方面的問題 If you are in financial difficulties.

（3）與其 rather...than..., not so much...as...

（4）而不是 rather than

（5）倒不如；滿可以 might just as well

（6）廉價 a bargain price, moderate prices

（7）轉譯：外食亦是一筆很大開銷 Eating/dining out is very expensive. The cost of eating/dining out is very high.

【譯文2】：If you have economic problems, there are various ways of saving your money. Instead of purchasing new apparel, you may try to purchase fashionable clothing in charity shops where second-hand items are sold. Dining out can also cost you enormously. Therefore, cooking with friends at home can be economically enjoyable. In addition, taking buses and taxies is also a considerable expense; thus, buying an affordable bicycle as a means of transportation seems to be a worthwhile alternative for a change.

【解析】：（1）詞性轉換：外食亦是一筆很大開銷 Dining out can also cost you enormously.

（2）既便宜又好玩 economically enjoyable

（3）重組：所以值得買一輛便宜的腳踏車代步

thus, buying an affordable bicycle as a means of transportation seems to be a worthwhile alternative for a change.

（4）增譯：in addition, for a change

（5）considerable, enormous, great, high, huge + cost

（6）considerable, enormous, great, vast, big, high + expense

a lot of expense

【譯文3】：If you have financial problems, various ways can save your money. Instead of wasting money on new clothes, you can try to find second-hand ones in charity stores where there are many fashionable products at fair price. Eating outside is also costly. Cooking with friends is money-saving and interesting. Taking buses and taxis also costs a lot, so it is worth buying a bicycle to commute.

【解析】："you" 主詞增譯，中文是兩句話用逗點隔開；英譯時，使用合句法，利用關係副詞連接兩句。

103年公務人員高等考試一級暨二級考試試題（第二版）

一、英譯中

題目1

【原文】：Standard Silicon Valley perks like cafeterias with free food, shuttle buses, gyms, ice cream parlors and dry cleaners not only make employees' lives easier, but keep them on campus during the day and promote contact with other employees. Nearly all tech companies have desks packed tightly together without walls and communal work areas with sofas and bean-bags.

【譯文1】：標準的矽谷津貼一應俱全，像是免費自助餐、接駁車、體育館、冰淇淋店、乾洗店等，不但讓員工生活更便利，也讓他們能夠整天都待在園區，能更有機會接觸其他同事。幾乎所有高科技公司皆把辦公桌排成一片，緊密相連，布置成共同工作區，除了擺設沙發，還附有豆袋坐墊。

【解析】：（1）perk 津貼；額外補貼

（2）增譯：一應俱全，排成一片。

（3）詞性轉換："contact" 英文為名詞，中文轉換為動詞。

【譯文2】：標準的矽谷公司就如自助餐廳，提供免費餐點、接駁車、健身中心、冰淇淋店和乾洗店，不僅讓員工生活更方便，也讓他們在工作的過程中，與其他同事有更多的互動。幾乎所有科技公司的桌子與桌子間緊靠且遠離牆面，公共工作區擺設沙發及豆袋椅。

【解析】：（1）增譯「提供」。

（2）"...not only..., ...but also..." 譯成「……不僅讓，……也讓……」。

題目2

【原文】：In recent years, gift-card commerce has become extremely profitable, which also explains why it has become susceptible to fraudulent activities. Here is an example of how the crime happens: A manager in a large company purchases gift cards for staff bonuses and bills them to the company expense account. But instead of actually passing the gift cards out, he takes them home. The manager was using gift cards to conceal corporate embezzlement.

【譯文1】：近年來，禮品卡商機無限，同時卻也容易遭受欺詐行為的影響。以下就是個犯罪發生的例子：某間大公司的經理買了禮品卡要當員工獎金，並開帳單向公司出納組報

帳，但他並未發出禮品卡，實際上卻私吞禮品卡。這位
經理正是用購買禮品卡的方式掩飾盜用公款的事實。

【解析】：（1）轉譯：gift-card commerce has become extremely profitable 禮品卡商機無限。

（2）be susceptible [sə`sɛptəbl] to 容易遭受；容易受……
的影響

（3）減譯：fraudulent activities [`frɔdʒələnt] 欺詐的；欺騙
的

（4）增譯：bills them to the company expense account 開帳
單向公司出納組報帳。

（5）重組：actually。

（6）embezzlement [ɪm`bɛzlmənt] 挪用；侵吞；盜用公款

【譯文2】：禮品卡商務近幾年來成為極易獲利的工具，這也是為什
麼它容易被用來作為詐騙手段，以下是一個案例。一家
大公司的經理買了一些禮品卡，當作是員工的獎金，並
記在公司的帳上。但他將禮品卡中飽私囊，而未發給員
工，所以他是利用購買禮品卡之名，行盜用公款之實。

【解析】：（1）省譯 "explains"。

（2）"how the crime happens" 從名詞子句省譯成名詞。碰
到"for" 與 "and" 就斷句，並視情況增譯。

二、中譯英

題目1

【原文】：微軟創辦人蓋茲、股神巴菲特、歌手史汀這三人有何共同
點？ 答案是他們都有大筆財富，卻沒全部留給子女。這
些超級富豪認為被金錢寵壞的孩子，如果可以隨意花用大
筆遺產，未來不會做聰明的選擇，無法過健全、有創造性
的生活。

【譯文1】：What is one thing in common among Gates－the founder of Microsoft, Buffett－the legendary stock-invester, and Sting－the topnotch singer? The answer is that even though they own an enormous fortune, not all the fortune is left to their children. These billionaires believe that those spoiled children, who have easy access to the tremendous heritage and spend the money with their free will, will neither make smart choices nor lead a healthy and creative life in the future.

【解析】：（1）增譯：Sting – the topnotch singer。

（2）可以隨意花用大筆遺產 who have easy access to the tremendous heritage and spend the money with their free will

（3）fortune：considerable, enormous, great, immense, large, substantial, vast small + fortune

（4）合併：這些超級富豪認爲被金錢寵壞的孩子，如果可以隨意花用大筆遺產，未來不會做聰明的選擇，無法過健全、有創造性的生活。These billionaires believe that those spoiled children, who have easy access to the tremendous heritage and spend the money with their free will, will neither make smart choices nor lead a healthy and creative life in the future.

【譯文2】：What do those people have in common; founder of Microsoft, Bill Gates, investment guru, Warren Buffett and the singer, Sting? The answer is that they all possess well fortune. Nonetheless, not all of their fortune were passed to their children. These wealthy people think spoiled children will not make wise choices if they can spend heritage without any control, not to mention living in a healthy and creative life.

【解析】：（1）「被金錢寵壞的」減譯成分詞形容詞 "spoiled"。
　　　　　（2）「隨意」翻成 "without any control"，正話反說。

　　題目2

【原文】：Oscar Pistorius*把他成功的動力歸功於他的母親。她從不
　　　　　因為他的殘障而給他特別待遇。她寫給他這樣的句子：
　　　　　「真正的輸家絕不是最後一個跑過終點線的參賽者。真正
　　　　　的輸家是坐在一旁的那位連比賽都不願意嘗試的人。」
　　　　　*提示Oscar Pistorius 南非籍殘障奧運田徑冠軍

【譯文1】：Oscar Pistorius attributed his motive power of success to his
　　　　　mother, who had never offered him special treatment even
　　　　　though he was physically handicapped. She wrote him a mes-
　　　　　sage like this which read, "A real loser is not the last contes-
　　　　　tant that crosses the finish line, but the one who would rather
　　　　　sit beside than give it a try."

【解析】：（1）詞性轉換：他的殘障 he was physically handicapped.
　　　　　（2）動力 motive power, motive force
　　　　　（3）「真正的輸家絕不是最後一個跑過終點線的參賽
　　　　　　　　者。真正的輸家是坐在一旁的那位連比賽都不願意
　　　　　　　　嘗試的人。」此句亦可翻譯成："A real loser is not
　　　　　　　　the last contestant that crosses the finish line, but the
　　　　　　　　one who would rather sit beside than give it a try."

【譯文2】：Oscar Pistorius attributed his success to his mother. She has
　　　　　never given him any privilege due to his disability. She wrote
　　　　　a sentence to him like this "a real looser is not the last contes-
　　　　　tant who runs through a finish line; a real looser is the person
　　　　　who sits aside and does not dare to give it a try.

【解析】：合併「Oscar Pistorius 把他成功的動力歸功於他的母親。

她從不因為他的殘障而給他特別待遇」。

103年公務人員特種考試外交領事人員及外交行政人員、國際經濟商務人員、民航人員及原住民族考試試題

一、英譯中：請將下面英文段落翻譯成中文。

【原文】：For as long as as Cambodian rice farmers can remember, their product has had an unsavory reputation. Tough, dirty and un-milled, it was impossible to cook evenly, and even farmers traded it as pig feed in exchange for cash or better-quality rice from Vietnam or Thailand. Even as other areas of agriculture flourished, rice production languished, a national embarrassment in a country where 80 percent of the population works in paddies. In 2009, Cambodia exported just 11,442 metric tons of milled rice, putting it at the bottom of the global heap. But as Thailand, one of the world's largest rice exporters, struggles with instability, Cambodian exports have improved along with their quality. Last year, Cambodia was the world's fifth-largest exporter of rice and the second-biggest exporter of premium jasmine rice. Sales of milled rice abroad reached 343,692 metric tons.

【譯文】：柬埔寨的稻農長久以來都記得，他們的產品名聲不佳。他們的農作物堅硬、骯髒、又未經研磨處理，不可能均勻煮熟，甚至農人把這些作物當作豬飼料來做交易，以換取現金或是來自越南或泰國更高品質的稻米。即便其他地區的農業興旺，稻米產量依舊沒有起色，對於有80%的人口從事農業的國家而言相對難堪。柬埔寨於2009年只輸出11,442公噸的碾磨後稻米，在全球國家中排在最後。就在全球稻米主要供應國泰國正面臨稻米收成不穩定之際，

柬埔寨的稻米輸出有所增長，品質也相對提升。柬埔寨是去年全世界第五大稻米輸出國，同時也是第二大主要香米供應的國家。碾磨後稻米的銷售在全球達到了343,692公噸。

【解析】：（1）for as long as sb. can remember = for a long time, throughout sb.'s memory 長久以來某人都記得

（2）unsavory [ʌn`sevərɪ]（令人）討厭的

an unsavory reputation 名聲不佳

（3）將同位語 "a national embarrassment in a country where 80 percent of the population works in paddies" 譯成句子。

（4）"have improved along with their quality" 使用分句法和增譯法，譯成「有所增長，品質也相對提升」。

二、中譯英：請將下面中文段落翻譯成英文。

【原文】：飛越大西洋的長途客機票價通常不便宜。然而專門在歐洲經營廉價飛航的「挪威穿梭航空公司」打算將它的低價經營模式拓展到美國及亞洲。挪威穿梭的策略採取了幾項不同於一般的做法：把長途航線的作業本部自挪威移到愛爾蘭，部分機組員駐在曼谷，在美國僱用空服員，同時採用最先進的波音787夢幻客機。這惹火了已有分量的同行及駕駛員。

【譯文】：The ticket price for long flights across Atlantic Ocean is usually not cheap. However, Norwegian Air Shuttle (NAS), specialized in managing low-cost carrier in Europe, is planning to expand its low-fare managing style to the United States of American and Asia. NAS adopted some strategies different from other ordinary ones：moving the main sector responsible for long trips from Norway to Ireland, locating parts of crew members in Bangkok, and employing flight attendants in the U.S. In the meantime, NAS adopted the state-of-the-art Boeing 787 Dreamliner. These actions provoked some people in the same profession and pilots who have weighty status in the industry.

【解析】：（1）「專門在歐洲經營廉價飛航的」，譯成形容詞子句。

（2）把「這」增譯成 "These actions"。

（3）「已有份量的」譯成形容詞子句。

（4）地位 position, place, status, standing

102年公務人員特種考試外交領事人員及外交行政人員考試

一、中翻英：請將下列句子翻譯成英文。

題目1

【原文】：我們展開可以幫助雙方降低彼此歧見、擴大共識領域的談話。

【譯文1】：We are holding talks for the purpose of helping decrease biases against each other and extending the sphere of consensus.

【解析】：（1）轉換：先翻譯 "We are holding talks" 然後翻譯 "for the purpose of"。

（2）增譯：for the purpose of 為了……目的。

（3）一致：共識 consensus

（4）領域 domain, territory, field, sphere

【譯文2】：We would hold a dialogue **that would help reduce differences between both sides and expand the common ground**.

【解析】：（1）改譯，由於中文形容詞太長，特按照英文習慣「尾重原則」將中文中修飾談話的形容詞改成形容詞子

句放到 "dialogue" 後面。

（2）expand 擴大；擴充；發展

題目2

【原文】：每次的成功，其實都只是讓我們拿到通往更棘手問題的門票。

【譯文1】：Each and every success, in fact, is merely an entrance ticket to a thornier problem.

【解析】：（1）增譯：each and every success。

（2）門票 an entrance ticket, an admission ticket

【譯文2】：Actually, each success is an admission ticket to a thornier problem.

In fact, each success is an admission ticket to a thornier problem.

As a matter of fact, each success is an admission ticket to a thornier problem.

【解析】：（1）改譯：將副詞「其實」從句子中提取出來，放在句首。

（2）其實 in fact, as a matter of fact, actually

二、英翻中：請將下列句子翻譯成中文。

【原文】：Far better is it to dare mighty things, to win glorious triumphs, even though checkered by failure than to rank with those poor spirits who neither enjoy much nor suffer much, because they live in a gray twilight that knows not victory nor defeat.

【譯文1】：比起只想過著安穩生活，不知人生苦樂的人來說，敢於冒險，縱使有時失敗，仍一路過關斬將，是再好不過的人生了！因為那些不知人生苦樂的人不明白勝利或失敗的滋味。

【解析】：（1）重組：Far better is it to dare mighty things, to win glorious triumphs than to rank with those poor spirits who neither enjoy much nor suffer much.... 英文句子是倒裝句，中文重整爲直述句。

（2）重組："to dare mighty things, to win glorious triumphs, even though checkered by failure" 翻成「敢於冒險，縱使有時失敗，仍一路過關斬將」。

（3）轉譯："those poor spirits who neither enjoy much nor suffer much" 翻成「不知人生苦樂」。

（4）拆句："because they live in a gray twilight that knows not victory nor defeat" 翻成因爲「那些不知人生苦樂的人不明白勝利或失敗的滋味」。

【譯文2】：與其處在生活渾渾噩噩不知勝敗之滋味的人群之中，**雖然這些人承受的很少，但是他們享受的也很少**，還不如去挑戰偉大的事情：儘管歷經挫折，但是會有光榮的勝利。

【解析】：（1）順序改譯，將原文 "Far better..." 前面好的品質放到後面，先說壞的品質。

（2）改譯："even though checkered by failure" 中的 "failure" 改譯爲「挫折」。

（3）增譯：將 "who neither enjoy much nor suffer much" 譯成讓步句「雖然……但是……」。

（4）改譯：將原文的比喻 "live in a gray twilight" 改成直譯「渾渾噩噩」。

（5）glorious [ˋglorɪəs] 光榮的，榮耀的；輝煌的

（6）triumph [ˋtraɪəmf] （大）勝利

（7）checker 使交錯；使盛衰無常；使交替變化；使多樣化

（8）rank 列隊

（9）twilight [ˋtwaɪˌlaɪt] 朦朧狀態；模糊狀態

102年公務人員高等考試一級暨二級考試試題

一、英翻中：請將下列英文翻成中文。

【原文】：Single-parent families currently account for only 7.6% of all households (560,000), but that proportion has grown by 50% over the last decade. The increase in single-mother families has been particularly pronounced：they account for 74% of households of this type, up from 65% a decade ago.

【譯文1】：現今所有56萬戶家庭中，目前單親家庭只占7.6%，但在過去10年，成長比例達到50%。而單親媽媽家庭的成長特別的顯著。這種家庭的成長比例從10年前的65%上升至目前的74%。

【解析】：（1）pronounced, marked, significant, massive, substantial 顯著的

增加：名詞 a pronounced/marked/significant/massive/ substantial increase

減少：名詞 a pronounced/marked/significant/massive/ substantial decrease

增加：動詞 to increase/rise/climb/improve
名詞 increase/rise/climb/improvement/upturn

減少：動詞 to decrease/fall/decline/worsen/downturn
名詞 decrease/fall/decline/worsening/downturn/ drop

形容詞 a slight/insignificant increase/decrease
a big fast/quick/sharp/dramatic/sudden increase/decrease
steady/moderate

副詞 a lot/sharply/dramatically/suddently/

【譯文2】：單親家庭現階段在所有的家庭中只占了7.6%，但這個比例在過去10年成長了一半。以母親為主的單親家庭不斷增加，此現象特別表示：「該模式在所有的家庭中，從10年前的65%增長到74%」。

【解析】："The increase in single-mother families has been particularly pronounced" 使用分句法及增譯法，譯成「以母親為主的單親家庭不斷增加，此現象特別表示」，是為了避免譯出不符合中文慣用語言表達方式的譯文（例：……的……的增長），其中「增加」在譯文轉換成動詞形式。

二、中翻英：請將下列中文翻成英文。

【原文】：健康減重必須找到新的生活平衡點，如改掉吃美食的習慣，或由開車通勤改成走路、騎腳踏車等，從生活作息的改變，減少熱量攝入、增加熱量消耗，才是根本之道。

【譯文1】：In order to lose weight healthily, we have to find a balance point in life, such as changing the habit of eating fancy food or replacing car commuting with walking and bicycling. It is the fundamental way out of obesity that we change our life-style, decrease the intake of calories, and increase the consumption of calories.

【解析】：（1）平衡點 a balance point, an equilibrium point
（2）增譯："It is the fundamental way out of obesity" 的 "obesity"。
（3）拆句：或由開車通勤改成走路、騎腳踏車等，從生活作息的改變。

【譯文2】：To lose weight in a healthy way, you need to find a balance point in your life. For instance, you can quit eating delicate

實用中英翻譯法

cuisine, or try to walk and ride a bike instead of driving. Changing your lifestyle, reducing intake of calories, and increasing consumption of calories are actually fundamental ways.

【解析】：（1）"you" 主詞的增譯。

　　　　　（2）「通勤」的省譯。

102年公務人員高等考試一級暨二級考試試題（第二版）

一、英翻中：請將下列英文翻成中文。

　　題目1

【原文】：Taiwan has long been held in high esteem for the level of its medicine. Medicine has become an important part of the international humanitarian aid provided by the Republic of China. The assistance is not only being provided on foreign soil but also at home in Taiwan. Throughout the year local hospitals are hosting visiting professionals from around the world who come to Taiwan to learn the latest medical techniques.

Patients from many different nations are also seeking treatment at Taiwanese hospitals in this age of borderless medicine.

【譯文1】：長期以來，臺灣醫術水準十分受到尊敬。醫術已成為中華民國所提供之國際人道救援時的重要一部分。除了向國外提供此援助之外，也提供國內此援助。臺灣當地醫院一整年致力於接待來自全世界來臺學習最近醫學技術的專家們。在此無國界醫術的世紀中，來自許多不同國家的患者也正在臺灣的醫院尋求治療當中。

【解析】：（1）in high esteem 十分尊敬

　　　　　（2）重組：Throughout the year local hospitals are hosting

visiting professionals from around the world who come to Taiwan to learn the latest medical techniques. 臺灣當地醫院一整年致力於接待來自全世界來臺學習最近醫學技術的專家們。

【譯文2】：臺灣長久以來因其醫學發達而有崇高的地位。醫學是中華民國提供的國際人道救援中不可或缺的部分，國內外都需要援助。這些年來，地方各醫院邀請來自全球各地的專業人士，來臺學習最新的醫學技術。在這個醫學無國界的世代，不同國家的患者也都來臺尋求醫療照顧。

【解析】：（1）「發達」為增譯。

（2）"important" 譯成「不可或缺的」，採用正話反說。

（3）The assistance is not only being provided on foreign soil but also at home in Taiwan.省譯成「國內外都需要援助」。

（4）"who come to Taiwan to learn the latest medical techniques" 採形容詞子句後置法，並以逗點隔開。

題目2

【原文】：In the wake of Taiwan's many years of rapid economic development, problems such as excessively long work hours and increasingly distant interpersonal and familial relationships are becoming issues for our society.

【譯文1】：臺灣迅速經濟發展多年之後，許多問題正成為我們社會的議題，如過度超時工作與愈來愈疏離的人際與家庭關係等問題。

【解析】：（1）in the wake of ... 繼……之後

（2）重組："problems such as excessively long work hours and increasingly distant interpersonal and familial relationships are becoming issues for our society." 許多問題正成為我們社會的議題，如過度超時工作與愈來愈疏離的人際與家庭關係等問題。

【譯文2】：在臺灣多年經濟蓬勃發展後，工時過長以及朋友和家人間的距離愈來愈遠等問題漸漸成為了我們社會中的議題。

【解析】：（1）"excessively long" 省譯成「過長」。

（2）"increasingly distant" 譯成「距離愈來愈遠」，皆採用詞性轉換，副詞轉形容詞以及形容詞轉名詞。

二、中翻英：請將下列中文翻成英文。

題目1

【原文】：人們認識客家人是因為他們的一些特質，比如說，客家人非常重視傳統和教育；而他們在艱難環境下努力工作的態度，也是為大家所熟悉的。當客家人移居到臺灣時，很多地方已經被當地人占據了，因此他們只能住在當地人不要的土地上，同時必須辛勤的工作才能存活。現在臺灣人口大約有15%是客家人，其中不乏成功有名的人。

【譯文1】：We get to know Hakka people because of some of their characteristics. For example, they place much importance on their tradition and education. In addition, their industrious attitude toward work under harsh conditions is also well known. Most of the land was occupied by the locals when Hakka people immigrated to Taiwan. Therefore, the Hakka people could only settle down in the rest of the areas unwanted by the locals, and at the same time, they needed to work diligently for their survival. Nowadays, approximately 15 percent of Taiwan's population is Hakka people. Among them, there is no lack of such people as some successful celebrities.

【解析】：（1）第一句 "We get to know Hakka people because of some of their characteristics." 也可以用下列強調句型翻譯。

強調句型：It is...that... 就是……

It is because of some of Hakka people's characteristics that we get to know them. 人們認識客家人正是因為他們的一些特質。

（2）重視 to value, to attach importance to, to place importance on, to make much of, to think highly of, to take sth. seriously, to pay much attention to, to take account of, to give weight to

（3）不乏其人 There is no lack of such people.

（4）拆句：當客家人移居到臺灣時，很多地方已經被當地人占據了，因此他們只能住在當地人不要的土地上，同時必須辛勤的工作才能存活。

Most of the land was occupied by the locals when Hakka people immigrated to Taiwan. Therefore, the Hakka people could only settle down in the rest of the areas unwanted by the locals. And at the same time, they needed to work diligently for their survival.

現在臺灣人口大約有15%是客家人，其中不乏成功有名的人。

Nowadays, approximately 15 percent of Taiwan's population is Hakka people. Among them, there is no lack of such people as some successful celebrities.

【譯文2】：Folks know about Hakka people because of their characteristics. For instance, Hakka people value tradition and education very much. In addition, the attitude they have when they make effort on work in severe environments is also well known by most of people. A lot of places had been occupied by locals after Hakka people migrated to Taiwan. Therefore, they could only live in places where locals would rather not live and had to work diligently in order to survive. Now, 15% of Taiwan's populations are Hakka people, including quite a few prestigious ones.

【解析】：（1）「他們在艱難環境下努力工作的」譯成一長形容詞子句"they have when they make effort on work in severe environments."。

（2）「當地人不要的」譯成關係副詞子句 "where locals would rather not live."。

題目2

【原文】：當人們享受便捷網路帶來的豐富生活，同時也必須深思過度依賴虛擬世界而衍生的種種惡果。聰明上網的關鍵就是「有所節制」。

【譯文1】：While people enjoy the affluence which easy access to the Internet can bring to their lives, they also have to mindfully deliberate upon the ill effects derived from excessive dependence on the virtual world. "Refraining from excessive use" of the Internet is the key to wise Internet access.

【解析】：（1）詞性轉換：「豐富的」轉譯為名詞 "affluence"。

（2）便捷網路 easy access to the Internet

（3）惡果 an evil consequence, a disastrous effect, ill effects

（4）轉譯：ill effects derived from excessive dependence on the virtual world. 過度依賴虛擬世界而衍生的種種惡果。

（5）深思 to think (or reflect) deeply, to ponder, to meditate, to contemplate

（6）過度依賴 excessive dependence on, overreliance on

（7）衍生 derive from

（8）重組：聰明上網的關鍵就是「有所節制」。"Refraining from excessive use" of the Internet is the key to wise Internet access.

【譯文2】：People have to ponder deeply over the consequences derived from excessively relying on virtual reality when enjoying the plentiful life accompanied by the convenience of the Internet. The key to being a wise Internet user is "learn to control."

【解析】：（1）「惡」省譯。

（2）「同時」省譯。

（3）「聰明上網」意譯成 "being a wise Internet user"。

101年公務人員特種考試外交領事人員外交行政人員考試

一、英譯中

題目1

【原文】：The government coalition collapsed amid budget bickering, so the Prime Minister tendered his resignation, but he'll stay on to head a caretaker government.

【譯文1】：聯合政府在編列預算時雙方僵持不下，導致最終垮臺收場，首相引咎辭職，但他將會留下來領導臨時政府。

【解析】：（1）增譯："The government coalition collapsed amid budget bickering" 增譯成「聯合政府在編列預算時雙方僵持不下，導致最終垮臺收場」。

（2）coalition [ˌkoəˋlɪʃən]（政黨、國家等）臨時結成的聯盟

（3）collapse [kəˋlæps] 崩潰，瓦解；（價格）暴跌；

（計畫等）突然失敗

（4）bicker [`bɪkɚ] 吵嘴；爭吵

（5）tender（正式）提出，提供

（6）caretaker government 臨時代理的政府

　　　a caretaker government 看守政府

【譯文2】：在預算的爭論之中，聯合政府陷入癱瘓，所以總理遞交
　　　　　了辭呈，但他仍將留任，領導代理政府。

【解析】：順序改譯："The government coalition collapsed amid budget
　　　　　bickering"，先翻譯 "amid budget bickering"，再翻譯 "the
　　　　　government coalition collapsed."。

【譯文3】：聯合政府因預算問題經歷一番脣槍舌戰，**進而導致其分
　　　　　崩離析**。所以總理遞出辭呈以示負責，但他依舊須帶領
　　　　　著這個「看守政府」**直到任期結束**。

【解析】：（1）增譯：「進而導致其分崩離析」。
　　　　　（2）增譯：文中沒有「負責」二字。
　　　　　（3）增譯：「直到任期結束」。

　　題目**2**

【原文】：Globalization is conducive to the exchange of information,
　　　　　but with the ubiquity of 3C products, personal communication
　　　　　has also irrevocably changed.

【譯文1】：全球化有利於資訊交流，但隨著3C產品的普及，個人的
　　　　　通訊也有著不可磨滅的改變。

【解析】：（1）詞性轉換 "has also irrevocably changed" 動詞
　　　　　　　　"changed" 轉譯為名詞「改變」。
　　　　　（2）is conducive [kən`djusɪv] to + N./Ving 有助的；有益
　　　　　　　　的；促成的
　　　　　（3）ubiquity [ju`bɪkwətɪ] 到處存在；無所不在；普遍存在

（4）irrevocably [ɪˋrɛvəkəblɪ] 不能取消地；不能撤回地

【譯文2】：全球化有助於信息交流，但由於普遍存在的3C產品，個人通信已發生了不可逆轉的變化。

【解析】：（1）詞性轉換："ubiquity" 名詞轉譯為形容詞「普遍存在的」。

（2）"changed" 動詞轉譯為名詞「改變」。

【譯文3】：全球化是相互傳遞資訊、彼此互通有無的好方法，但隨著3C產品的普及，人們之間的溝通方式也隨之改變了。

【解析】：（1）增譯：「彼此互通有無的好方法」。

（2）減譯：「溝通方式也隨之改變」沒有翻出 "irrevocably"。

二、中譯英

題目1

【原文】：油價飆漲而經濟停滯。經濟不景氣的問題歸咎於高風險借貸和不動產泡沫化。

【譯文1】：Soaring oil prices led to economic stagnation. People imputed the problem of economic recession to high-risk loans and immovable property bubbles.

【解析】：（1）增譯：「led to, people」。

（2）soar [sor] 猛增；暴漲

（3）導致……後果 lead to, bring about, result in, give rise to, cause,

（4）不景氣 depression, recession, slump

（5）不動產 immovables, realty, immovable property, real estate

（6）歸咎於…… to impute...to..., to ascribe the blame to...

【譯文2】：Soaring oil price brought about economic stagnation, while economic downturn was attributed to loans of high risk and real estate bubbles.

【解析】：（1）改譯：原文沒有擬人效果，直接表述因果，譯文用
　　　　　　到 "brought about"。

　　　　　（2）改譯：將原文中的形容詞「高風險」，變成後置的
　　　　　　形容詞 "of high risk"。

　　　　　（3）改譯：主動句改爲被動句 "economic downturn was
　　　　　　attributed to...."。

　　　　　（4）bring about 引起，造成

　　　　　（5）downturn [`daʊnˌtɝn]（經濟）衰退，下降

　　　　　（6）ascribe...to..., attribute...to... 歸因於
　　　　　　be attributed to 把……歸因於；把……歸咎於

【譯文3】：The economy was bogged down due to the fact that the oil
　　　　　price was soaring up. And the recession could be attributed to
　　　　　high-risk loans and the burst of real estate bubbles.

【解析】：（1）be/get bogged down 使陷入泥沼；使陷於困境
　　　　　（2）due to the fact that 因爲

　　　題目2

【原文】：敘利亞持續動盪不安，2011年2月聯合國祕書長介入斡旋
　　　　　提出停火協議要求敘利亞政府與反政府軍隊於4月10日起
　　　　　停火，然而該日過後雙方仍有交火發生。

【譯文1】：In response to incessant waves of insurrection in Syria, the
　　　　　Secretary General of the United Nations intervened in Febru-
　　　　　ary 2011 to mediate a truce, demanding Syrian government
　　　　　and the anti-government rebels to cease fire as from April
　　　　　10th. However, constant crossfire between both sides had still
　　　　　been reported since then.

【解析】：（1）詞性轉換：持續動盪不安 incessant waves of insurrection

（2）增譯：in response to 作為對……的答覆

（3）主被動句轉換：然而該日過後雙方仍有交火發生。
Constant crossfire between both sides had still been reported since then.

（4）動盪不安 turbulence, pendulum, turmoil, commotion, disturbance, tumult, disorder, insurrection

（5）動盪不安的 turbulent, pendulous, in a turmoil

（6）祕書長 Secretary General

（7）休戰協定 a truce

（8）停火協議 cease-fire

（9）（指某事物開始的時間或日期）從……起 as from

（10）交火 crossfire

【譯文2】：With continuous turmoil in Syria, Secretary General of the United Nations intervened in mediation and proposed a truce in February 2011, demanding that both Syrian government troop and rebels should cease fire as from April 10th, but crossfire still went on after that date.

【解析】：（1）改譯：原文中「介入斡旋提出停火協議」改成了 "proposed a truce in his mediation and intervention"。

（2）介入 to intervene, to interfere, to step in, to get between, to wade into

（3）斡旋 to mediate, to intercede, to intervene

（4）斡旋（名詞）mediation, intercession, intervention

【譯文3】：With Syria in continuous turmoil, the Secretary General of the United Nations intervened in mediation and put forward the cease-fire agreement in Frbruary, 2001, demanding the Syrian government and the anti-government army to cease fire as from April 10th. However, the cross fire had been still reported since then.

【解析】：（1）停火；停火協議 cease-fire

（2）提出；提議 put forward

（3）提出 to bring up (an idea, etc.), to bring sth. in, to address, to put forward, to advance

101年公務人員高等考試一級暨二級考試試題

一、英譯中

題目1

【原文】：Skillful composers have long used silence to build a sense of anticipation. Some of music's finest moments are spent in transition－waiting, in essence, for the other shoe to drop. The snapshots of this pause may have implications beyond concert halls. They shine a light into what neuroscientists call "segmentation processes"－the techniques used by the brain to take a stream of sensory information and parcel it up into more easily comprehended pieces.

【譯文1】：熟練的作曲家長期以來使用寂靜以營造期待感。過渡更是有些好樂章精華之所在，本質上是在等待下一個樂章出現。這種稍稍停頓的簡要印象，對於音樂會大廳之外也可能有含意存在。這些簡要印象展露出一道曙光，也就是神經科學家所謂的「分割過程」，它是一種技巧，就是藉由大腦讓感官資訊流互相串連一體，產生出讓人更容易理解的音樂作品。

【解析】：（1）俚語：to wait for the other shoe to drop 將行動或決定延期，直到另一件事情結束或解決。

（2）movement【音】樂章；速度；拍子

（3）snapshot 簡要印象；點滴的了解

127

（4）transition 過渡；【音】臨時轉調；轉調過渡段

（5）重組：Some of music's finest moments are spent in transition－waiting, in essence, for the other shoe to drop. 過渡更是有些好樂章精華之所在，本質上是在等待下一個樂章出現。

【譯文2】：長久以來，經驗豐富的作曲家都會運用沉默來製造一種滿懷期待之感。有的樂曲中，最佳的瞬間往往是銜接的時刻──等待、靜候下一個美好時刻的到來。除音樂廳之外，這種停頓的瞬間在其他領域也別有含意。這些停頓便是神經學家所謂的分割程序──一種大腦執行的技術，擷取一連串的感知資訊後，將它組織成較易理解的訊息。

【解析】：（1）把 "long" 拉出來單獨翻譯，增譯成「長久以來」。

（2）把 "music" 拉出來單獨翻譯，增譯成「有的樂曲中」。

（3）利用中文常用逗號的特性，將一長句斷句。

題目2

【原文】：For many firms that do business in Europe, the certification of their recycling processes from the International Standards Organization is a must-have. Toxic materials such as lead, mercury and other heavy metals are used liberally in electronic devices, and burying them in landfills poses a future hazard if the metals leak into groundwater. While European countries have stringent recycling regulations, government mandates in the United States are less demanding. In America, large corporations are at the forefront in pushing for electronics recycling.

【譯文1】：對許多在歐洲經商的公司而言，在物料回收的過程，取

實用中英翻譯法

得ISO國際標準認證是不可或缺的條件。因為像鉛、汞與其他重金屬這種有毒的物質，都為電子零件設備所大量使用，然而往往業者事後將其傾倒至地層，如果這些物質滲透到地下水的話，未來可能會造成偌大的威脅。縱使歐洲國家在回收上都有嚴苛的規章，然而美國政府的命令在這方面就較無此高要求。在美國，往往都是大公司扮演著回收電子零件的主要推手。

【解析】：（1）增譯：

"and burying them in landfills poses a future hazard if the metals leak into groundwater." 然而往往業者事後將其傾倒至地層，如果這些物質滲透到地下水的話，未來可能會造成偌大的威脅。

（2）a must-have 不可或缺的條件

（3）at the forfront of... 在……的最前列

（4）轉譯：主要推手。

【譯文2】：要在歐洲設廠經營，國際標準組織認可的回收程序證明是絕對必要的。鉛、汞以及其他重金屬有毒物質常用來製造電子裝置，如果帶至垃圾掩埋場處理，金屬物質滲進地下水可能會對未來有所危害。儘管歐洲國家都有嚴格的控管規範，美國政府當局在這一環節卻不如歐洲。在美國，許多大公司都致力於推動電子裝置回收工作。

【解析】：（1）"are used liberally in" 以意義被動的概念譯成「常用來」。

（2）「工作」的增譯。

二、中譯英

【原文】：2005年，世界衛生組織報告指出，8%的成人是肥胖的，該組織也預測肥胖症會持續上升，甚至超越傳染疾病，成為人類嚴重的健康問題。能夠解釋全球肥胖症上升的因素，包括現代加工食品的增加、速食和垃圾食物的普遍。不過，諷刺的是，經濟進步是造成肥胖的主要原因，因為它帶給大眾都市化的生活、久坐不動的辦公室工作，和減少運動量的洗滌機、車輛與電子媒體。

【譯文1】：In 2005, a report from World Health Organization (WHO) indicated that eight percent of adults were obese. WHO also predicted that the obesity would continue to increase and the uprising obesity-related diseases would surmount the infectious deseases and turn out to be severe health problems of humans. The factors that explain this global uprising obesity consist of the increase of the modern processed food and the prevalence of fast food or junk food. Nonetheless, what is ironic is the fact that main cause of obesity is the economic progress as it brings people a metropolitan life, the office job sticking to the desk all day long, the washing machine that keeps people from exercise, vehicles, and electronic media.

【解析】：（1）拆句：2005年，世界衛生組織報告指出，8% 的成人是肥胖的，該組織也預測肥胖症會持續上升，甚至超越傳染疾病，成為人類嚴重的健康問題。

In 2005, a report from World Health Organization (WHO) indicated that eight percent of adults were obese. WHO also predicted that the obesity would continue to increase and the uprising obesity-related diseases would surmount the infectious deseases and turn out to be severe health problems of humans.

（2）超越 to surmount; to transcend; to surpass; to overtake; to get beyond

（3）增譯：諷刺的是……What is ironic is the fact that...。

【譯文2】：In 2005, a report from World Health Organization indicated that 9.8% of adults in the world are obese. It also predicted that the rate of obesity will keep rising and even surmount that of infectious diseases, becoming a serious health problem for human. The factor which can offer explanation of the rise of global obesity rate includes the increase of modern processed food and fast food. However, what's ironic is that advanced economy is the main reason of causing obesity because it brings people urbanized lifestyles, office work which people need to sit for a long time. Washing machines, vehicles and electronic media could also reduce the possibility for people to go exercising.

【解析】：（1）"the rate of" 為增譯。

（2）將「增加」和「普遍」合譯成 "increase"。

（3）「和減少運動量的洗滌機、車輛與電子媒體」增譯成一句話。

100年公務人員特種考試民航人員、外交領事人員及國際新聞人員

一、英譯中

題目1

【原文】：We face an enemy of ruthless ambition, unconstrained by law or morality. The terrorists despise other religions and have defiled their own.

【譯文】：我們面對的敵人，不僅野心殘暴，更是目無法紀，枉顧道德倫常，這群人就是恐怖分子，他們鄙視其他的宗教，如此也褻瀆了自己的信仰。

【解析】：（1）增譯：不僅……，更是……，枉顧……，這群人就是恐怖分子

（2）詞性轉換："face" 動詞轉譯爲形容詞「面對的」。

（3）"ruthless ambition" 翻譯成「野心殘暴」。

（4）"unconstrained by law or morality" 翻譯成「目無法紀，枉顧道德倫常」。

（5）ruthless ['ruθlɪs] 無情的；殘忍的

（6）unconstrained [ˌʌnkən`strend] 不受約束的

（7）defile [dɪ`faɪl] 汙染；玷汙

題目2

【原文】：Taiwan's business people are uniquely poised to draw on the mainland's talents and resources to bolster the fortunes of the people on Taiwan.

【譯文】：臺灣的企業慧眼獨具，拉攏大陸人才，善用大陸資源，正是爲了鞏固臺灣人民的財富。

【解析】：（1）轉譯："Taiwan's business people" 原意爲「臺灣的商人」，轉譯爲「臺灣的企業」。

（2）轉譯："uniquely poised" 原意爲「獨特地；泰然自若」，轉譯爲「慧眼獨具」。

（3）增譯："draw on" 原意爲「依靠」，增譯爲「拉攏」與「善用」。

（4）拆句：英文原句爲一句，中文拆成四句。

（5）mainland ['menlənd] 大陸

（6）uniquely [ju`niklɪ] 獨特地；唯一地

（7）poised [pɔɪzd] 泰然自若的

（8）draw on 依靠；利用；動用

（9）bolster ['bolstɚ] 支撐；加固；援助；支持

二、中譯英

題目**1**

【原文】：美國尼克森總統在1972年大陸之旅簽署了上海公報，這是開啓了中共資本主義改革之門的三份公報中，第一份也是最重要的公報。

【譯文】：During his journey to mainland China in 1972, the U.S. President Nickson signed up a Shanghai communiqué. It was the first one of the three communiqués, which was also the most important one that led to a prelude to the reform of the capitalism of mainland China.

【解析】：（1）重組：按照英文主詞＋動詞的句法順序，先翻譯「在 1972 年大陸之旅」，然後翻譯「美國尼克森總統」、「簽署了上海公報」。

（2）拆句：中文原文一句，英文翻譯拆成二句。

（3）轉譯：「開啓」英文翻成 "led to"。

（4）大陸 mainland China, Chinese mainland, the mainland

（5）簽約；簽署；簽名 sign up

（6）公報 communiqué [kəˌmjunəˋke]

（7）導致……後果 lead to

（8）前奏；序幕 prelude [ˋprɛljud]

題目**2**

【原文】：要餵飽預期在 2025 年接近 80 億的人口，整個世界需要加倍生產食物並且改善糧食的分配。

【譯文】：To feed up the expected global population of nearly eight billion in 2025, the entire world needs to double food production and amend the scheme of food distribution.

【解析】：（1）詞性轉換：動詞「生產」翻譯成名詞 "production"。

（2）轉譯：改善。

（3）增譯：「改善糧食的分配」翻譯成 "amend the scheme of food distribution"，增加了 "scheme"。

（4）養肥：養壯 feed up

（5）修訂；修改；訂正改進；改善 amend [ə`mɛnd]

（6）計畫：方案 scheme [sk`im]

100年公務人員高等考試一級暨二級考試試題

一、英譯中：請將下列英文譯為中文。

　　題目**1**

【原文】：Playing defense against Mainland China's rapidly emerging capitalist economy may well lessen the appeal of Taiwan as an investment destination.

【譯文】：對於中國大陸快速崛起的資本主義經濟，臺灣若設防的話，很可能會減少臺灣作為投資地的吸引力。

【解析】：（1）playing defense against... 對於……設防

　　　　　（2）拆句：一句拆成三句。

　　題目**2**

【原文】：Despite the amazing technological advances of our time, no invention can compare to the complex inner workings of the human body.

【譯文】：儘管我們時代驚人的發展，沒有一項發明可以和人體複雜的內部運作相提並論。

【解析】：compare to... 把……比作

二、中譯英：請將下列中文譯為英文。

　　題目**1**

【原文】：沒有一種以知識為基礎的經濟可以不為創作者提供充分的

保護，卻仍能有光明的前景。

【譯文1】：There is no such thing as the knowledge-based economy that has bright prospects without people providing the creators of the economy with sufficient protection.

【解析】　：（1）光明的 bright, promising

（2）前景 prospects

【譯文2】：The knowledge-based economy cannot have bright prospects without people providing the creators of the economy with sufficient protection.

【解析】　：（1）省譯「沒有一種」。

（2）cannot...without... 沒有（或缺乏）……就不行

【譯文3】：None of the knowledge-based economies can have bright prospects without providing creators with adequate protection.

【解析】　：光明的前景 bright prosects, a bright future

　　題目2

【原文】　：傳染性疾病乃因細菌或病毒散布所致，這些病原體會以各種不同的途徑進入體內。

【譯文1】：The epidemics are caused by the spreading of the viruses and bacteria. These pathogens can enter our body through various gateways.

【解析】　：（1）順譯。

（2）病原體 pathogen, a pathogenic organism

【譯文2】：The spreading of the viruses and bacteria can result in the epidemics. These pathogenic organisms can enter our body through a variety of pathways.

【解析】　：導致 lead to; bring about; result in; cause; give rise to

【譯文3】：The spread of bacteria and viruses lead to contagious diseases.

These pathogens intrude human bodies through various paths.

【解析】：（1）重組：傳染性疾病乃因細菌或病毒散布所致。The spread of bacteria and viruses lead to contagious diseases.

（2）傳染性疾病 infectious disease, contagious disease

100年公務人員高等考試一級暨二級考試試題（第二版）

一、英譯中：請將下列英文譯為中文。

題目1

【原文】：In today's world, we face many stressful situations that trigger the same fight-or-flight response. The difference is, these stresses are in large part emotional rather than physical in nature. In other words, we don't face many dangerous animals while driving to work nowadays, but we do face long hours on the job, financial struggles, family squabbles, and other troubling situations.

【譯文】：身處現今世界中，我們常常面臨壓力大的情況，而引起我們選擇奮鬥或是逃避的反應。不同的是，本質上，這些壓力大部分是情緒方面的壓力而不是生理方面的壓力。換言之，我們無須擔心上班途中會遭受極具危險動物的攻擊，但卻要面臨長時間的工作、財務困境、家庭紛爭或其他麻煩等的窘境。

【解析】：增譯：情緒方面的壓力而不是生理方面的壓力。我們無須擔心上班途中會遭受極具危險動物的攻擊。

題目2

【原文】：China outstrips India in almost every sphere of development except software. It attracts a bigger chunk of foreign investment, and its share of world exports, whether textiles or toys, is far bigger.

【譯文】：除了軟體之外，中國幾乎在每個發展領域都勝過印度。中國也吸引了更多外資，在紡織或玩具的世界的出口占有率也更多。

【解析】：重組：中國幾乎在每個發展領域都勝過印度。

二、中譯英：請將下列中文譯為英文。

題目1

【原文】：不到幾秒鐘的時間，竊賊就取下這幅畫，迅速地奔向地下室。在那裡他把這幅舉世聞名的人像畫從畫框拆下來，藏在他的油漆工作服裡，然後平靜的走向出口。

【譯文】：In less than a few seconds, the thief took the painting off the wall and rushed to the basement as fast as he could, where he dismantled the portrait of its frame and hid it in his painting outfit, and then quitetly walked toward the exit.

【解析】：（1）增譯：as fast as he could

（2）合併：where he dismantled the portrait of its frame

（3）重組：where he dismantled the portrait of its frame and then quitetly walked toward the exit.

題目2

【原文】：在漫長的執業生涯裡，屬於高風險群的醫師可能會被控告執業過失，但這些訴訟官司大都不會成功。

【譯文】：During the very long career of the medical practice, the vast majority of high-risk doctors may be sued for malpractice; however, these lawsuits are mostly unsuccessful.

【解析】：（1）被控告 be sued for

（2）however 的用法：However H大寫，另起一句英文；或 h 小寫，前面分號，後面逗號（; however,）

99 年公務人員高等考試一級暨二級考試試題

一、英譯中

題目1

【原文】：The most common form of insomnia is learned insomnia, in which a few sleepless nights lead to anxiety about being unable to get to sleep, making it even harder to do so. However long it lasts, insomnia is not a disease in itself but a symptom of another problem, or several problems, whether physical, emotional, or behavioral.

【譯文】：最常見的失眠類型就是透過經驗獲得的失眠，其中連續幾個晚上，輾轉難眠，焦慮不已，擔心自己無法入睡，殊不知，在此情況下更難入睡。不管失眠持續多久，失眠本身不是病，而是其他問題或幾個問題引起的症狀，無論是生理的、情緒的，或是外在行為的問題。

【解析】：（1）learned [ˋlɝnɪd] 透過學習（或經驗等）獲得的
　　　　　（2）in which 其中
　　　　　（3）增譯：「其中連續幾個晚上，輾轉難眠，焦慮不已，擔心自己無法入睡，殊不知，在此情況下更難入睡。而是其他問題或幾個問題引起的症狀」。

題目2

【原文】：Attitudes of respect, modesty and fair play can grow only out of slowly acquired Skills that parents teach their children over many years through shared experience and memory. If a child reaches adulthood with recollections only of television, Little League and birthday parties, then that child has little to draw on when a true test of character comes up, say, in a prickly business situation.

【譯文】：唯有父母多年身教言教，耳濡目染之下，方可慢慢培養小孩學習尊重、謙卑及公平競爭的態度。若兒時記憶僅止於看電視、聊少棒、跑生日派對，那麼小孩在成年時，比如說，在棘手的商務情境中，人格將備受考驗，小孩則是無所適從，面臨重重難關。

【解析】：（1）增譯："shared experience and memory" 身教言教，耳濡目染之下面臨重重難關

　　　　　（2）詞性轉換：看電視、聊少棒、跑生日派對。

　　　　　　　if a child reaches adulthood 在成年時

　　　　　（3）重組：比如說，在棘手的商務情境中，人格將備受考驗。

二、中譯英

題目1

【原文】：在現代化資本與知識密集的產業發展趨勢下，財富與所得分配的集中乃為難以迴避的必然結果。政府的重分配機制是民眾期盼社會公平正義的最後依靠，其中租稅制度尤為關鍵。

【譯文】：With the development trend of modernistic capital and knowledge-intensive industry, the centralization of wealth and income distribution turns out to be an inevitable consequence. The redistribution mechanism of the government is the people's ultimate dependence on which the public expects the government to carry out social fairness and justice, in which the land tax and other levies play a crucial role, in particular.

【解析】：（1）租稅制度 the system of land tax and other levies

　　　　　（2）增譯："unequal centralization"。

　　　　　（3）省譯：難以迴避的必然結果 an inevitable consequence

（4）重組：「政府的重分配機制是民眾期盼社會公平正義的最後依靠」。The redistribution mechanism of the government is the people's ultimate dependence on which the public expects the government to carry out social fairness and justice.

題目2

【原文】：兩性平權是建立在相互尊重與合作的架構上，而不是女權主義的高漲或兩性間的對立。只有兩性和諧共處，社會與國家才能安定。

【譯文】：Gender equality is not built on feminism upsurge or male-female conflicts but on mutual respect and cooperation. Only through agreeable interaction between men and women can the society and the nation be peaceful.

【解析】：（1）高漲 an upsurge, a wave, a surge, an upswing

（2）重組：Gender equality is not built on feminism up-surge or male-female conflicts but on mutual respect and cooperation.

（3）倒裝句：Only through...can + S.

Only through agreeable interaction between men and women can the society and the nation be peaceful.

99 年公務人員高等考試一級暨二級考試試題（第二版）

一、英譯中

【原文】：Crops produced through genetic engineering are the only ones formally reviewed to assess the potential for transfer of novel traits to wild relatives. When new traits are genetically engineered into a crop, the new plants are evaluated to ensure that they do not have characteristics of weeds. Where biotech crops are grown in proximity to related plants, the potential for the two plants to exchange traits via pollen must be evaluated before release. Crop plants of all kinds can exchange traits with their close wild relatives (which may be weeds or wildflowers) when they are in proximity. In the case of biotech derived crops, the Environmental Protection Agency (EPA) and U.S. Department of Agriculture (USDA) perform risk assessments to evaluate this possibility and minimize potential harmful consequences, if any.

【譯文】：透過基因工程所製造的農作物是唯一以前複審的農作物，以評估將新特性移轉到野生近緣種的可能性。當這些基因新特性要藉由基因工程導入農作物時，新的植物必須經過評估，以確保新植物沒有雜草的特徵。由於這些生物科技農作物，生長之處通常都會與近緣種接近，植物間可能會透過花粉互換基因特性，因此發表該項技術前，必須要事先經過審慎評估。當所有種類的農作物接近時，都可能跟它自己的野生近緣種（可能是野草，也可能是野花）互相交換特性。這種藉由生物科技所生產的作物的事例，環境保護局與美國農業部決定大膽試驗，評估其可能性，並降低任何可能造成的不良後果。

【解析】：（1）potential [pə`tɛnʃəl] 可能性；潛力，潛能

　　　　　（2）weeds 雜草；野草

　　　　　（3）proximity [prɑk`sɪmətɪ] 接近，鄰近

　　　　　（4）related 有親緣關係的；同一類型的

　　　　　（5）重組：Where biotech crops are grown in proximity to related plants, the potential for the two plants to exchange traits via pollen must be evaluated before release.

（6）release [rɪˋlis] 發行；發表

（7）由於這些生物科技農作物，生長之處通常都會與近緣種接近，植物間可能會透過花粉互換基因特性，因此發表該項技術前，必須要事先經過審慎評估。

（8）harmful 有害的；不良的

（9）Crop plants of all kinds can exchange traits with their close wild relatives (which may be weeds or wildflowers) when they are in proximity. 當所有種類的農作物接近時，都可能跟它自己的野生近緣種（可能是野草，也可能是野花）互相交換特性。

（10）in proximity 接近；鄰近

二、中譯英

【原文】：臺灣農業屬小農家庭農場經營形態，提升競爭力最大的限制在於農戶眾多且經營規模小，兼業比率過高，研發成果商品化不足，欲求降低產銷成本及導入現代化、企業化經營管理及行銷頗為不易。若能藉由建立農業中心衛星體系，推動農業經營企業化，將可有效整合小農成為大農，並以產銷組織間的專業分工、資源互補，來加速生產結構改善，提高產銷效率，進而發展高值、高效農業，強化競爭優勢。

【譯文】：Agriculture in Taiwan belongs to a management mode of a small family farming. The biggest limitations of upgrading its competitiveness lie in the small-scale operation with a number of farmers, excessive ratio of part-time farming, and deficiency in commercialization of research and development achievement. It is very difficult to reduce the cost of production and marketing and to lead in modernization and enterprise management and marketing. If we can establish a satellite system of agricultural center to promote the running of enterprise of agricultural management, then we can effectively integrate small farmers into large ones. In addition, we can use professional division of labor between production and marketing organization and complementary resources in order to expedite the improvement of production structure to increase the efficiency of production and marketing, and then to develop high-value and high-efficiency agriculture and strengthen competitive advantages.

【解析】：（1）經營形態 management model, management mode, management style

（2）在於 lie in

（3）研發 research and development

（4）商品化 commercialization

（5）企業化 be run/operated as an enterprise

（6）整合 integrate...into, incorporate...into

（7）分工 division of labor

（8）互補 complement；互補的 complementary

（9）加速 speed up, to accelerate, to hasten, to precipitate, to expedite

（10）提高 to lift, to raise, to heighten, to enhance, to increase, to improve, to advance

（11）進而 and then

（12）強化 to strengthen, to intensify, to consolidate, to underline, to tone up

（13）拆句：臺灣農業屬小農家庭農場經營形態，提升競爭力最大的限制在於農戶眾多且經營規模小，兼業比率過高，研發成果商品化不足。Agriculture in Taiwan belongs to a management mode of a small family farming. The biggest limitations of upgrading its competitiveness lie in the small-scale operation with a number of farmers, excessive ratio of part-time farming, and deficiency in commercialization of research and development achievement.

98 年公務人員特種考試外交領事人員及國際新聞人員考試

一、英譯中：請將下列英文譯為中文。

題目1

【原文】：Few forces on earth are more powerful than an active volcano. Yet in 1973, the residents of a small island in Iceland managed to curb one that threatened to destroy their town and only harbor. The eruption on the island of Heimaey began on the morning of January 23. Within a few hours, nearly the entire population of the island had been evacuated by sea or air.

【譯文】：活火山的破壞力是地球上其他天然災害無可比擬的。然而1973年時，冰島一座小島上的居民曾設法遏止一座活火山，其破壞力能將整座城鎮夷為平地，島上唯一的港口也難以倖免。海明威島上的火山於1月23號的早晨開始爆發。幾個小時內，幾近整個島嶼的居民皆由陸海空撤離避難。

【解析】：（1）增譯："force" 增譯為「其他天然災害」。

"destroy their town and only harbor" 增譯為「將整座城鎮夷為平地，島上唯一的港口也難以倖免」。

（2）詞性轉換："threaten" 動詞轉譯為名詞「破壞力」。

（3）轉譯：Few forces on earth are more powerful than an

active volcano. 轉譯爲「活火山的破壞力是地球上其他天然災害無可比擬的」。

（4）重組：nearly the entire population of the island had been evacuated by sea or air. 重組譯爲「幾近整個島嶼的居民皆由陸海空撤離避難」。

（5）force [fors]【物】力；力的強度

（6）manage to 成功的完成，設法

（7）curb [kɝb] 控制，遏止

（8）eruption [ɪˋrʌpʃən]（火山）爆發

（9）evacuate [ɪˋvækjuˌet] 撤空，撤離；從……撤退

題目2

【原文】：American intelligence agencies have concluded in recent months that Iran has created enough nuclear fuel to make a rapid, if risky, sprint for a nuclear weapon. But new intelligence reports delivered to the White House say the country has deliberately stopped short of the critical last steps to make a bomb.

【譯文】：近幾個月，美國情報單位推斷，伊朗爲了大量製造核武，在短期內冒著風險生產了足夠的核燃料。然而從白宮新的情報顯示，該國因缺乏製造核武器的重要步驟，而愼重地停止該計畫。

【解析】：（1）重組：Iran has created enough nuclear fuel to make a rapid, if risky, sprint for a nuclear weapon. 先翻譯 "to make a rapid, if risky sprint for a nuclear weapon."，然後翻譯前面的 "has created enough nuclear fuel"。伊朗爲了大量製造核武，在短期內冒著風險生產了足夠的核燃料。

（2）轉譯："bomb" 根據前後文將 "bomb" 轉譯爲核武器。

（3）conclude [kənˋklud] 推斷出；斷定

（4）sprint [sprɪnt] 短時間的劇烈工作

（5）deliberately [dɪˋlɪbərɪtlɪ] 愼重地；謹愼地

二、中譯英：請將下列中文譯爲英文。

題目1

【原文】：網路科技愈來愈發達，資訊取得較以前更爲容易，想知道某個人的消息，只要在Google等網路搜尋引擎打上幾個關鍵字就可略知一二，甚至連廣告行銷也以此爲賣點，火紅了好一陣子。

【譯文1】：The network technology has become more prevalent, which makes information more easily accessible/available than before. If you want to know someone's information, just enter a few keywords into Google search engine and you may know a thing or two about it. Even advertisement marketing utilizes this as a selling spot. The phenomenon has gone viral for a while.

【解析】：（1）重組：「資訊取得較以前更爲容易」此句以英文形容詞子句翻譯。

（2）轉譯：「發達」轉譯爲 "prevalent" [ˋprɛvələnt] 流行的，盛行的；普遍的。

（3）發達 prospering, prosperous, advanced, developed, prevailing, prevalent, popular

（4）accessible [ækˋsɛsəbl] 可（或易）接近的

（5）available [əˋveləbl] 可用的，可得到的

（6）比以前 than before, than ever, than ever before

（7）略知一二 have slight knowledge of, have a smattering of, have a rough idea, know a little, know something about, understand a little about, know a thing or two about, get an inkling of

（8）賣點 selling spot; selling point

（9）爆紅 go viral

　　This video has gone viral on YouTube. 這個影片已經在 YouTube 上爆紅。

【譯文2】：With the increasing popularity of Internet technology, information is more easily accessible than ever. If you want to know someone's information, you may have slight knowledge of it as long as you enter some keywords into some search engines such as Google. This selling point is even employed in advertisement marketing, which has gone viral for a while.

　　題目2

【原文】：臺灣今年5月中旬受邀以觀察員身分出席第62屆世界衛生大會（WHA），這是臺灣退出聯合國38年後首次參與聯合國體系的正式會議。

【譯文】：Taiwan was invited to attend the sixty-second World Health Assembly (WHA) as an observer in mid-May this year. It has been thirty eight years since Taiwan withdrew from the United Nations, so this was the first time for Taiwan to participate in the official conference hosted by the UN.

【解析】：（1）拆句：中文有一句，英文拆成二句。

　　　　　（2）出席 attend

　　　　　（3）退出 to withdraw from, to drop out, to sign off, to make one's exit, to exit, to secede, to retreat

　　　　　（4）參與 participate in, take part in, partake in

98 年公務人員高等考試一級暨二級考試試題

英譯中：將下列英文句子翻譯成爲中文。

　　題目1

【原文】：Only recently have biologists started to learn how plants work.
　　　　　They found the ways plants synchronize their flowering with
　　　　　the state of the environment. During the time of flowering,
　　　　　plants are particularly vulnerable to environmental stresses.

【譯文】：直到最近，生物學家才開始得知植物生長過程。他們發
　　　　　現，植物會依環境狀況而調整開花期。尤其到了開花階
　　　　　段，植物則會受制於環境壓力，顯得特別脆弱。

【解析】：（1）改譯："how plants work" 爲「植物生長過程」。
　　　　　（2）省譯："ways"。
　　　　　（3）增譯：尤其到了開花階段，植物則會受制於環境壓
　　　　　　　　　力，顯得特別脆弱。

　　題目2

【原文】：Some scientists claim that progress in delaying aging will
　　　　　come in the next decades. Although halting the aging process
　　　　　completely is far beyond the understanding of science, most
　　　　　researchers agree that preserving physical function is more
　　　　　important than just increasing life span.

【譯文】：某些科學家聲稱，10年之後，延緩老化的進展即將來臨。
　　　　　雖然停止老化的過程科學無法完全理解，但大部分的研究
　　　　　人員同意，保留生理機能遠比增加壽命重要的多。

【解析】：（1）decade [ˋdɛked] 10年
　　　　　（2）in the next decades 數十年之後
　　　　　（3）beyond understanding 無法理解

（4）重組：雖然科學無法完全理解停止老化的過程。

（5）life span 壽命

98 年公務人員高等考試一級暨二級考試試題（第二版）

英譯中：將下列英文句子翻譯成為中文。

題目1

【原文】：With the bringing up of the price of coal and natural gas, the payback periods have been shortened for renewable energy plans. All over the world, solar energy is on the verge of huge development. A forecast issued in 2008 indicated solar power will develop from a $25 billion industry in 2007 to $80 billion in 10 years.

【譯文】：隨著燃煤與天然氣的價格上漲，這些物料的回收期已縮短，因應可回收再利用的能源計畫。世界各地都一樣，太陽能瀕臨極大的發展。根據2008年發布的一項預測，該能源工業在10年內，也就是從2007年開始將快速發展——從幣值250億上升到800億。

【解析】：（1）with the... 隨著……

（2）on the verge of... 接近於……；瀕臨……

（3）增譯："for renewable energy plans" 增譯為「因應可回收再利用的能源計畫」。

（4）拆句：A forecast issued in 2008 indicated solar power will develop from a $25 billion industry in 2007 to $80 billion in 10 years. 根據2008年發布的一項預測，該能源工業在10年內，也就是從2007年開始將快速發展——從幣值250億上升到800億。

題目**2**

【原文】：The Chinese consider calligraphy a way of keeping one healthy. One of the reasons is that it involves the exercise of the hand, the entire body, and the mind. Calligraphy is so abstract and sublime that in Chinese culture a scholar's penmanship is often regarded as his most revealing trait.

【譯文】：中國人認為練書法是保持健康的一種方式。其中的一個原因是它包含了手部、全身與心智的運動。書法的意境相當抽象與宏偉，所以在中國文化，學者們的筆跡通常被認為能透露出其真性情。

【解析】：（1）增譯："calligraphy" 為「練書法」。

（2）involve 牽涉；需要，包含，意味著

（3）增譯："Calligraphy is so abstract and sublime" 為「書法的意境相當抽象與宏偉」。

（4）詞性轉換："in Chinese culture a scholar's penmanship is often regarded as his most revealing trait" 為「所以在中國文化，學者們的筆跡通常被認為能透露出其真性情」。

（5）penmanship [`pɛnmənˌʃɪp] 書寫；書法；字跡，筆跡；寫作；寫作風格；文體

題目**3**

【原文】：This is an important age of Intellectual Property. Many companies have been built around patented technology. Patent filings and issuance are skyrocketing. According to the spirit of the copyright and patent laws, everything made by man is patentable.

【譯文】：現在是智慧財產權的重要時代。許多公司爭相申請科技專

利。專利的申請和發布也隨之猛漲。根據著作權及專利法
的精神，任何人類所創造之物皆可享有專利。

【解析】：（1）被動轉主動：Many companies have been built around
patented technology. 許多公司爭相申請科技專利。

（2）skyrocket [`skaɪˌrɑkɪt] 猛漲；突然高升

97年公務人員特種考試外交領事人員外交行政人員及國際新聞人員考試試題

一、英譯中：請將下列英文譯為中文。

題目1

【原文】：The widely expected slowdown in the expansion of world
output and trade turned out to be much stronger than most
observers had projected at the beginning of the year 2001.
Global output increased only marginally and world trade de-
creased somewhat, both developments in sharp contrast to the
preceding year when both trade and output expanded at record
rates. (WTO Annual Report, 2002)

【譯文】：全球產量及貿易日益擴增，雖然各界皆預測會出現衰退趨
勢，但衰退程度卻超乎觀察家在2001年初所推測的結果。
全球產量只有小幅成長，反觀全球貿易卻小幅下跌；前一
年產量與貿易成長趨勢皆勢如破竹，與今年之表現形成強
烈對比。（WTO年度報告，2002年）

【解析】：（1）expansion [ɪk`spænʃən] 擴展；擴張

（2）output 產量

（3）slowdown [`sloˌdaʊn] 衰退

（4）turn out to be（後接名詞或形容詞）結果是……；原
來是……；證明是……

（5）project [prə`dʒɛkt] 預計，推斷，預測

151

（6）observer [əb`zɝvɚ] 觀測者；觀察員

（7）in sharp contrast to 強烈對比

（8）preceding [prɪ`sidɪŋ] 在前的

（9）record 空前的；創紀錄的

題目2

【原文】：For the purpose of enabling each State, as far as practicable under the conditions in such State, to furnish financial assistance to aged needy individuals, there is hereby authorized to be appropriated for each fiscal year a sum sufficient to carry out the purposes of this title. (US Social Security Act)

【譯文】：為了讓各州能提供財務援助給有需要的老人，只要是每州可實行的情況下，財政部已獲准每會計年度撥出足夠款項實行此一計畫。（美國社會安全法）

【解析】：（1）增譯：「財政部」。

（2）省譯："to carry out the purposes of this title" 譯為「實行此一計畫」，省譯 "purposes"（目的）、"title"（標題）。

（3）for the purpose of 為了……的目的

（4）practicable [`præktɪkəbl] 能實行的，行得通的

（5）furnish [`fɝnɪʃ] 供應；提供

（6）appropriated [ə`proprɪˌet] 撥出（款項等）＋ for

（7）fiscal year【美】會計年度；財政年度

（8）carry out 實行，執行，進行

二、中譯英：請將下列中文譯為英文。

題目1

【原文】：統治國家的權力屬於人民全體，不是個人、不是政黨。這是「自由意志」的充分發揮，是「主權在民」的完全落

152

實，是眞正的「順乎天，應乎人」，眞正的革故鼎新。一切的榮耀，歸於所有的人民。

【譯文】：The power of sovereignty over a nation belongs not to individuals or polical parties, but to the general public, which thoroughly embodies the gist of "free will" and the complete realization of "sovereignty of the people": a true innovative reform that describes the idea of "obeying the will of Heaven and being in harmony with people". All glories are ascribed to the people.

【解析】：（1）重組：「屬於人民全體，不是個人、不是政黨」譯爲 "belongs not to individuals or political parties, but to the general public"。

（2）詞性轉換：「充分發揮」爲 "thoroughly embodies the gist"。

（3）合併："which thoroughly embodies the gist of 'free will' and... "。

（4）增譯："gist"。

（5）充分發揮 bring...into full play

（6）sovereiegnty [ˋsɑvrɪntɪ] 統治權[(+ over)]

（7）embody [ɪmˋbɑdɪ] 體現；使具體化

（8）gist [dʒɪst] 要點；主旨

（9）be ascribed [əˋskraɪbd] to... 把……歸屬（於）

題目2

【原文】：若非當初臺灣銀行界爲了競爭消費金融的誘人利潤，幾乎沒有限制地擴張授信額度，現在也不會有一個月收入不過26,000元的上班族竟然會負債一兩百萬。

【譯文】：If Taiwan's banking community had not unrestrictedly expanded credit limit in order to compete for attractive profits of consumer finance in the first place, there would not have been a phenomenon that office workers, who earned less than NT$26,000 a month, slipped into debt of one or two million dollars.

【解析】：（1）增譯：in the first place, a phenomenon

（2）銀行界 banking circles, banking community, banking world

（3）上班族 white-collar worker, office worker

（4）負債 in debt

（5）slip into debt, slip 不知不覺地陷入[(+into)]

（6）與過去事實相反的假設句：

If S. + had p.p. ... , S. + would/should/could/might have + p.p.

96 年公務人員特種考試外交領事人員及國際新聞人員考試試題

中譯英：請將下列中文段落譯成英文，英文段落譯成中文。

題目1

【原文】：索羅門群島（the Solomon Islands）於本（96）年4月2日發生強烈地震並引發海嘯，造成43人死亡，逾千人受傷的慘重災情。中華民國（臺灣）政府本諸「人溺己溺」之人道精神，立即透過我駐索國大使館捐贈20萬美元予索政府賑災。此外，由外交部與衛生署共同設立之跨部會任務編組 Taiwan IHA 亦同時組派醫療隊，並攜帶200餘公斤藥品於4月5日趕赴索國，在災情最嚴重之吉佐島（Ghizo Island）架設醫療站，與各國際救援組織並肩救援。

【譯文】：A violent earthquake occurred on the Solomon Islands, followed by a tsunami, causing a disastrous calamity of forty three deaths and more than a thousand casualties on April 2nd, 2007. The Taiwanese government, in accordance with the humanistic spirit of "putting oneself in somebody else's shoes", immediately donated US$ 200,000 in aid of the Solomon government for disaster relief via the Taiwan Embassy in Solomon. Besides, Taiwan IHA, an inter-departmental task force, co-established by the Department of Foreign Affairs and the Department of Health, not only dispatched a team of the medical staff who carried over 200 kilograms of medicine to the Solomon on April 5th and set up the medical station on Ghizo Island, but also teamed up with other international rescue organizations for rescue shoulder to shoulder.

【解析】：（1）重組：可以先翻譯結果，再翻譯原因。

Forty three people died and more than a thousand people were wounded in a severe earthquake, followed by a tsunami, which occurred on the Solomon Islands on April 2nd, 2007.

（2）合併：not only dispatched a team of the medical staff who carried over 200 kilograms of medicine to the Solomon on April 5th.

（3）發生 happen, occur, take place, break out

a. **happen** 強調的是事情的偶發性或意外性

e.g., What's happening?

b. **occur** 用法比 "happen" 正式一些，通常用於有明顯意義的主詞後，像是自然現象或是科學現象之後。"occur" 經常與副詞一起出現，表示物體或事件的存在，發生或出現等。

e.g., On the morning of 22 March 2016, three coor-dinated nail bombings occurred in Belgium：two at Brussels Airport in Zaventem, and one at Maelbeek/Maalbeek metro station in Brussels.

c. take place 用於經過預定、計畫的事件上

e.g., The concert will take place next Wednesday.

d. break out 使用在突然發生（爆發）的火災，戰爭，疾病等災難性事件，如："The Second World War broke out on 1 September 1939"。不過，日常生活對話中更常用的習慣用法是 "There was a big earthquake last night"。而書報雜誌上則常用 hit 或 strike 等動詞，表示襲擊之意，如："A big earth-quake hit/struck Hokkaido last night." 昨天北海道發生了大地震。

e.g., The Second World War broke out on 1 Septem-ber 1939.

（4）強烈地震 violent earthquake, severe earthquake, strong earthquake

（5）海嘯 tsunami [tsuˋnɑmi]（源自日語）

（6）傷亡人員 casualities [ˋkæʒjʊəltɪz]

（7）受傷的 wounded [ˋwundɪd], injured

（8）慘重災情 disastrous calamity

（9）本諸 in accordance with, in accord with

（10）人溺己溺 put onelsef in someone's shoes, in some-one's shoes

（11）設身處地 to place (or put)oneself in others' position

（12）為了幫助（或救濟）…… in aid [ed] of...

（13）賑災 disaster relief

（14）派遣 dispatch [dɪ`spætʃ]

（15）與……合作 team up with

（16）跨部會的 inter-departmental

（17）任務編組 task force, task group

（18）並肩 shoulder to shoulder, side by side

題目2

【原文】：In times of hostility, diplomats are often withdrawn for reasons of personal safety, as well as in some cases when the host country is friendly but there is a perceived threat from internal dissidents. Ambassadors and other diplomats are sometimes recalled temporarily by their home countries as a way to express displeasure with the host country. In both cases, lower-level employees still remain to actually do the business of diplomacy.

【譯文】：戰爭時，政府會將外交官召回，往往是爲了他們的人身安全，或有時候態度友善的東道國，卻察覺有來自內部持不同政見者的威脅。有時候祖國也會將外交大使與外交官暫時召回，作爲表達對東道國不滿的一種方式。若遇到上述兩種情況，一般外交雇員仍要持續上班，處理實際外交事宜。

【解析】：（1）增譯："for reasons of personal safety" 增譯爲「往往是爲了他們的人身安全」。

（2）被動轉主動："diplomats are often withdrawn" 轉爲「政府會將外交官召回」。

（3）轉譯："low-level employees" 轉譯爲「一般外交雇員」。

（4）hostililty [hɑs`tɪlətɪ] 敵意；敵視；戰爭行動；戰爭；戰鬥

（5）host [host] country 主人；東道主

（6）dissident [ˋdɪsədənt] 持不同政見者

（7）ambassador [æmˋbæsədɚ] 大使；使節

（8）home country 祖國

（9）displeasure [dɪsˋplɛʒɚ] 不快；不滿；生氣

95 年公務人員特種考試外交領事人員考試試題

一、中譯英：請將下列各句中文譯為英文。

　　題目1

【原文】：一群住在倫敦的農人宣稱，牛的叫聲是有地域性口音的。
　　　　　對這樣的說法，語音學者們認為並不離譜。不過，需要科
　　　　　學研究來進一步證實。

【譯文】：A group of British farmers living in London claim that the
　　　　　sounds of cows have regional accents. Phonetic experts indi-
　　　　　cate that this claim is not too far stretched. However, it still
　　　　　needs to be verified by further scientific research.

【解析】：（1）詞性轉換：「牛的叫聲是有地域性口音的」轉為
　　　　　　　　 "the sound of cows has regional accents"。

　　　　　（2）離譜的 too far stretched; too far out; far away from
　　　　　　　　 what is normal; far off the beam

　　題目2

【原文】：近日來從英國飛往美國的飛機受到炸彈威脅，造成了班機
　　　　　延誤及手提行李受到限制，也讓富裕的商務乘客考慮選擇
　　　　　私人旅行，為私人包機提高了商機。

【譯文】：Flights from the UK to the United States of American have
　　　　　been under threat of bombs these days, which has caused
　　　　　flight delays and carry-on luggage restrictions. Thus, many

實用中英翻譯法

rich business passengers take the option of personal journey into consideration, thereby increasing the business opportunity of personal chartered airplane.

【解析】：（1）重組：近日來 "these days" 置於句末。

（2）受到炸彈威脅 under threat of bombs

（3）考慮 consider, take...into consideration/account

（4）私人包機 chartered airplane

二、英譯中：請將下列各段英文譯成中文。

題目1

【原文】：The Second World War was the war of global conferences. Air travel made it possible for the wartime leaders and their aides to meet and discuss informally the problems of mutual concern. Twice Churchill crossed the Atlantic to meet Roosevelt, once in Washington in 1941, once in Quebec in 1943. Later in November of that year Chiang Kai-shek flew to Cairo to confer with Roosevelt and Churchill on Far Eastern strategy and two days later the British and the American leaders met with Premier Stalin at Teheran.

【譯文1】：第二次世界大戰是一場全球會議的戰爭。因航空之便，使得戰時領袖和其隨從得以會面與非正式的討論共同關切的問題。邱吉爾曾經兩次橫跨大西洋與羅斯福會面，一次在1941年的華盛頓，一次則是在1943年的魁北克。後來在該年的11月，蔣介石飛往開羅與羅斯福和邱吉爾商討遠東策略的問題，而兩天後，英國和美國領袖在德黑蘭與史達林總理會面。

【解析】：（1）轉譯："Air travel made it possible" 轉譯為「因航空之便」。

（2）重整：Twice Churchill crossed the Atlantic to meet Roosevelt, once in Washington in 1941, once in Quebec in 1943. 邱吉爾曾經兩次橫跨大西洋與羅斯福會面，一次在1941年的華盛頓，一次則是在1943年的魁北克。

【譯文2】：第二次世界大戰是全球互抗的戰爭，空中旅行使得戰爭時期領導者和其同盟國能夠非正式地見面，及討論相互關心的議題。邱吉爾兩次飛過大西洋去見羅斯福，一次是1941年在華盛頓，另一次則是1943年在魁北克。稍後在同年的11月，蔣中正飛抵開羅與邱吉爾、羅斯福商討遠東戰略，而在兩天之後，英美兩國領袖則是和史達林總理在德黑蘭相見。

【解析】：增譯：關心的議題。

題目2

【原文】：To bring equality of opportunity and more freedom to his people, Dr. Martin Luther King, Jr., a young black Baptist minister, fought segregation in buses in Montgomery, Alabama; and in schools, jobs, and housing all over the U.S.. He told people about his "dream of equality...a dream of a land where men will not argue that the color of a man's skin determines the content of his character."

【譯文1】：為了給人民帶來機會平等和更多自由，一個年輕的浸信會黑人牧師馬丁·路德·金恩博士，反對在阿拉巴馬州蒙哥馬利市的公車上實行乘坐隔離制度，以及全美學校中、工作與住宅的隔離制度。他曾經告訴人們有關其對「人人平等的夢想……夢想擁有一塊淨土，沒有人會爭論說一個人的膚色會決定其人格的內容」。

【解析】：（1）fight segregation 反對隔離
　　　　　（2）重組與增譯："fought segregation in buses in Mont-
　　　　　　　　gomery, Alabama" 譯為「反對在阿拉巴馬州蒙哥馬
　　　　　　　　利市的公車上實行乘坐隔離制度」。
　　　　　（3）增譯："segregation" 為「隔離制度」。
　　　　　（4）增譯："a dream of a land" 為「夢想擁有一塊淨土」。

【譯文2】：馬丁路德‧金博士是一位年輕的黑人牧師，他為了他的
　　　　　同胞們要來爭取更多自由和平權，他在前往蒙哥馬利郡
　　　　　途中的公車上極力對抗那不公不義的種族隔離制度，然
　　　　　後他將此活動的觸手伸至校園、工作場合及家家戶戶之
　　　　　中。為的就是要告訴人們一個有關「追求自由」的夢，
　　　　　而這個夢是述說著一個沒有用膚色來決斷一人的內在和
　　　　　個性的地方。

【解析】：（1）重組：「馬丁路德‧金博士是一位年輕的黑人牧師，
　　　　　　　　他為了他的同胞們要來爭取更多自由和平權」。
　　　　　（2）增譯：「活動的觸手」。

94 年公務人員特種考試外交領事人員考試試題

一、中譯英：請將下列各句中文譯為英文。

　　題目1

【原文】：7月份於倫敦發生的兩波炸彈攻擊，已引發英國一連串新
　　　　　的反恐措施。英國首相Tony Blair說：「遊戲規則已經開
　　　　　始改變。」

【譯文】：The occurrence of two waves of bomb attacks in London in
　　　　　July has triggered a series of new anti-terrorism measures.
　　　　　"Rules of the game have begun to change." said Tony Blair,
　　　　　the U.K. Prime Minister.

【解析】：（1）增譯："the occurrence"。

（2）重組：「7月份於倫敦發生的兩波炸彈攻擊」譯為 "The occurrence of two waves of bomb attacks in London in July"。

（3）重組：英國首相Tony Blair說：「遊戲規則已經開始改變。」

"Rules of the game have begun to change." said Tony Blair, the U.K. Prime Minister.

（4）引發 initiate, trigger, touch off

引起 trigger off

引起：造成 bring about

題目2

【原文】：表面語言形式的不同是否意味著內在思維模式的不同？還是外顯行為及信念差異或許只是人類相同心智的不同外在表情而已？

【譯文】：Does the difference in superficial language forms signify the difference in the internal thought patterns? Or is it likely that the external behaviors and differences in belief imply the diversely external appearance of humans' identical minds?

【解析】：（1）意味 signify, imply

（2）重組：「表面語言形式的不同」重整譯為 "the difference in superficial language forms"。

（3）相同的 identical, the same, alike, like, similar, equal, equivalent, parallel

（4）不同的 different, distinct, diverse, dissimilar

二、英譯中：請將下列各句英文譯為中文。

題目1

【原文】：English may have transformed the world, but with non-native

實用中英翻譯法

speakers now outnumbering native speakers 3 to 1, the language is being reshaped in return. In Asia alone, the number of English users has topped 350 million, roughly the combined populations of the United States, Britain and Canada.

【譯文】：縱使英文可能已改變了整個世界，但現在非母語與母語人士所占的比例是3：1，反而讓這個語言趨勢重新洗牌。就單單拿亞洲地區來說，講英文的人數已超過3億5千萬人，大概是整個美國、英國跟加拿大加起來一樣多。

【解析】：（1）增譯：「縱使」、「反而」、「語言趨勢」。

（2）reshape [ri`ʃep]（使）再成形；重新塑造；改造

（3）in return 回報；交換

（4）top 高出；超越

題目2

【原文】：The world is changing in every conceivable dimension, such that humanity is faced with a new scheme of being. Policymakers can choose to ignore these developments and be swept along with them in mindless confusion or they can seek to understand them and explore better coping mechanisms that may enable public institutions to maintain some measures of control and direction.

【譯文】：無論是從哪一個面向而言，世界都正在改變，以至於人性正面臨著全新的整合與改革。而政策制定者可以選擇無視這些發展，囫圇吞棗並隨波逐流，抑或者試著去了解，去探索出更適當的處理機制，這或許能夠讓公家單位好好維持一些管控與方向的措施。

【解析】：（1）conceivable [kən`sivəbl] 可想到的；可想像的

（2）dimension [də`mɛnʃən] 方面

（3）重組："The world is changing in every conceivable dimension" 重組譯爲「無論是從哪一個面向而言，世界都正在改變」。

（4）a new scheme of being 新的本質／存在系統／體制／結構

（5）轉譯："be swept along with them" 轉譯爲「隨波逐流」。

sweep 沖走；席捲

（6）轉譯："in mindless confusion" 轉譯爲「囫圇吞棗」。

（7）confusion [kən`fjuʒən] 困惑；慌亂

（8）mindless [`maɪndlɪs] 沒頭腦的；愚蠢的

94 年公務人員高等考試一級暨二級考試試題

一、英譯中：請將下列英文譯爲中文。

題目1

【原文】：In the new digital age, viewers themselves will become creators and distributors of their own video content. Mom and Dad could film Junior playing ball in the backyard, then send the clip over the Internet to Grandma, who'll watch it on a high-definition, interactive TV alongside her evening news.

【譯文1】：在現今的新數位時代裡，觀眾自己也將會變成創作者與分享者來分享他自己的影片內容。父母們可以拍自己孩子在後院玩球的影片，然後將短片上傳至網路，供遠端正用著高解析互動式電視看著晚間新聞的祖母觀賞。

【解析】：重組：Grandma, who'll watch it on a high-definition, interactive TV alongside her evening news. 遠端正用著高解析互動式電視看著晚間新聞的祖母觀賞。

【譯文2】：在數位新時代，每個人皆可錄製並分享自己獨特的視頻。像父母可以拍攝孩子們玩耍的畫面，並透過網路就能讓祖父母觀看高畫質新聞，同時享受天倫之樂。

【解析】：減譯、詞性轉換。

題目2

【原文】：Viewer-created content might even go mass market. During the recent tsunami in Asia, news organizations often ran pictures ordinary people had posted on Web sites. News Corp. founder Rupert Murdoch predicted that bloggers using text, sound, and video would eventually take the place of some of the reporters working for him.

【譯文1】：素人自拍的影片也能讓普羅大眾看到。在南亞大海嘯之際，許多新聞組織在網絡上播放著由大眾所拍攝的照片。新聞媒體公司的創辦人Rupert Murdoch預測一些使用打字、音檔和影片的部落客終將會取代若干在他旗下工作的記者們。

【解析】：（1）增譯「素人」。
　　　　　（2）mass market 面向大眾

【譯文2】：由觀眾自行上傳的影片，可能在大眾媒體市場蔚為風潮，尤其是最近亞洲發生的大海嘯，許多新組織紛紛掃視那些圖集，大部分都來自網路上普羅大眾，新聞集團的創辦人，魯柏·梅鐸預測善用文字、聲音與影片的部落客，最後可能取代他旗下工作的記者。

【解析】：增譯、詞性轉換。

題目3

【原文】：The next generation wants control over their media instead of being controlled by it. The growth of digital media will give us that control－we'll be able to watch whatever we want, whenever we want, screening out anything that's not of interest, and even creating our own private channels. Will it make us better informed and entertained? Or simply more isolated?

【譯文1】：下一代的人們想要掌控他們自己的媒體而不是被其掌控。數位媒體的成長茁壯將會讓我們更快達到這個目標，我們將能看任何我們想看的節目，在任何一個時候觀看，而且將我們不感興趣的內容摒除，甚至於創立專屬於我們自己的頻道。而這樣一來，真的有辦法讓我們得到更多知識和娛樂嗎？或是只是讓我們更加孤單而已呢？

【解析】：（1）增譯："The growth of digital media will give us that control" 譯為「數位媒體的成長茁壯將會讓我們更快達到這個目標」。

（2）改譯：改變詞性。"Will it make us better informed and entertained?" 譯為「真的有辦法讓我們得到更多知識和娛樂嗎？」。

【譯文2】：我們的下一代應該要讓人民掌控媒體，而不是受制於它。如今數位媒體日新月異，愛你所看，看你所選，甚至開創私人頻道。如此的發展究竟是讓民眾知識及娛樂性一手掌握抑或與社會脫節呢？

【解析】：增譯、詞性轉換。

二、中譯英：請將下列各句中文譯為英文。

題目1

【原文】：不同觀點的人聚在一起時，便互相質疑做事的方法和思考的習慣。

【譯文1】：When the people holding different views get together, they

will question each other about how other people work and
think.

【解析】：（1）增譯：holding 持有……（觀點：意見）

　　　　　（2）質疑 call in question, query, harbor suspicions

　　　　　（3）省譯：「做事的方法和思考的習慣」譯爲 "how
other people work and think"。

【譯文2】：The moment people with different perspectives joined a gath-
ering, they tended to question each other concerning their way
of coping and the pattern of thinking.

【解析】：直譯。

　　題目2

【原文】：成功團隊的共通點是都有幾位有經驗的成員。

【譯文1】：One thing in common in a successful team lies in the fact that
there are several experienced members.

【解析】：轉譯：有 lie in

【譯文2】：All successful teams have a shared reason behind their suc-
cess－a couple of veteran team members.

【解析】：直譯。

　　題目3

【原文】：我們都必須對一些非常複雜的議題做出困難的決定。

【譯文1】：We have to make difficult decisions for those complex issues.

【解析】：重組：「對一些非常複雜的議題做出困難的決定」譯爲
"make difficult decisions for those complex issues"。

【譯文2】：We must make hard decisions on some extremely complex issues.

【解析】：直譯。

91年公務人員特種考試外交領事人員考試第一試試題

一、英譯中：請將下列英文譯成中文。

題目1

【原文】：In the interests of regional security, Taiwan's ruling DPP has refrained from making overt moves toward independence despite party ideology.

【譯文】：此舉雖有違政黨意識形態，但基於地區安全考量，執政的臺灣民進黨已不再公然採取臺獨行動。

【解析】：（1）in the interest of 為某事物的緣故

in the interest of regional security 為了地區安全

（2）增譯：「此舉雖有違政黨意識形態但基於地區安全考量」。

（3）改譯：改變詞性。"overt" 改譯為副詞「公然地」。

題目2

【原文】：Japanese Prime Minister Junichiro Koizumi yesterday expressed deep remorse for Asian victims of the nation's aggression during World War II as Tokyo commemorated the 57th anniversary of its surrender.

【譯文】：就在昨日，日本政府在東京舉行了第二次世界大戰之後第57週年投降紀念日，日本首相小泉純一郎表示，對於因日本入侵亞洲而受害的難民，深表懊悔。

【解析】：（1）增譯：「日本政府」。

（2）拆句：英文為一句，中文拆成多句。

（3）重組：就在昨日。

（4）改譯：將動詞 "commemorated" 改譯為名詞「紀念日」。

題目**3**

【原文】：The government will shift its defense strategy to beef up the Navy's defense capability and procure more battleships and minesweeping helicopters after bolstering Taiwan's Air Force in the past decade.

【譯文】：過去這10年來，臺灣全力培養空軍實力，而接下來，政府將改變防禦策略以增強海軍防禦能力，並增購更多戰艦及掃雷直升機。

【解析】：（1）增譯：「臺灣全力培養空軍實力」。

　　　　　（2）defense 防禦；保衛；防護

　　　　　（3）beef up 增強；加強

　　　　　（4）重組：「過去這10來……」。

　　　　　（5）bolster 支撐；加固；援助；支持

　　　　　（6）procure [proˋkjʊr]（努力）取得，獲得；採辦；為……獲得

　　　　　（7）minesweeper [ˋmaɪnˌswipɚ] 掃雷艦

二、中譯英：**請將下列中文譯成英文。**

題目**1**

【原文】：總之，我們絕不能把國家的前途，完全仰賴於美國的全力支持，更不能把人民的安全，完全寄望於中共能自我節制。

【譯文1】：To sum up, neither the future of our nation nor the safety of our people can be dependant on the full support of the United States and self-restraint of mainland China.

【解析】：（1）重組：neither...nor...

　　　　　（2）合併：中文多句譯為一句。

【譯文2】：To sum up, we cannot rely on the full support of the United

States for the future of our nation. Nor can we rely on the self-restraint of mainland China for the safety of our people.

【譯文3】：To sum up, we cannot rely on the full support of the United States for the future of our nation, let alone rely on the self restraint of mainland China for the safety of our people.

【解析】：（1）仰賴 to rely on, to be dependant on

　　　　　（2）總之 to sum up, in summary, in short, in a word, in any case, in sum, in brief, briefly

　　　　　（3）「更別提；更不用說；而且還……」否定意味。

　　　　　　　　a. let alone + V./N.，通常用於帶否定意味的句子後。

　　　　　　　　b. not to mention / to say nothing of / not to speak of + N/Ving。

　　　　　　　　c. still less / much less + V./N.，否定意味的句子，意指「更別提；更不用說」。

　　　　　（4）「更別提；更不用說；而且還……」肯定意味。

　　　　　　　　still more / much more + V./N.，肯定意味的句子，意指「而且還……」。

　　題目2

【原文】：游揆強調，中華民國有不得不走出去的壓力，所以這次出訪的目的是突顯中華民國存在的事實，讓國際間看得見臺灣。

【譯文】：Premier Yu（游揆）emphasized that under tremendous pressure, the Republic of China cannot help but face the issue of internationalization. As a result, the purpose of this visit was to accentuate the fact of ROC's existence in order for Taiwan to nudge its way onto the international stage.

【解析】：（1）增譯："under tremendous pressure"。

（2）拆句：「所以這次出訪的目的是突顯中華民國存在的事實，讓國際間看得見臺灣」（"As a result..."）。

（3）轉譯：「走出去」轉譯爲 "face the issue of internationalization"。

（4）轉譯：「讓國際間看得見臺灣」轉譯爲 "in order for Taiwan to nudge its way onto the international stage"。

（5）突顯 accentuate; stress; emphasize; punctuate; underline focus attention on; bring/call/draw attention to; point up

（6）輕推 nudge [nʌdʒ]

（7）不得不

cannot but + V

cannot help but + V

cannot choose but + V

can do nothing but + V

have no choice/ option/ alternative but + to V

cannot help + Ving

題目3

【原文】：「覆巢之下無完卵」，面對中共的各種打壓行動，我們全體同胞應誓爲政府的後盾，共同努力開創新的外交活動空間。

【譯文】："A collapsed country harbors no intact homes." In face of various forms of suppressive actions from mainland China, we, as Taiwan's compatriots, should vow to rally our support behind the government in a joint effort to create a new diplomatic arena.

【解析】：（1）轉譯：「覆巢之下無完卵」譯爲 "A collapsed country harbors no intact homes."。

（2）拆句：「覆巢之下無完卵」，面對中共的各種打壓行動 "In face of ...."。

（3）harbor [ˋhɑrbɚ] 庇護

3-6 教育部中英文翻譯能力檢定考試試題與解析

100 年教育部中英文翻譯能力檢定考試試題

英譯中一般文件筆譯類（一）

【原文】：**A Formula for Economic Calamity**

The market crash of 2008 that plunged the world into the economic recession from which it is still reeling had many causes. One of them was mathematics. Financial investment firms had developed such complex ways of investing their clients' money that they came to rely on arcane formulas to judge the risks they were taking on. Yet as we learned so painfully three years ago, those formulas, or models, are only pale reflections of the real world, and sometimes they can be woefully misleading.

It was the supposed strength of risk models that gave investment firms the confidence to leverage their bets with massive sums of borrowed money. The models would tell them how risky these bets were and what other investments would offset that risk. Yet the huge uncertainties in the models gave them false confidence.

With so much at stake, in the past three years financial firms have spent tens of millions of dollars in buttressing their models of investment risk in the hope that new ones will preclude anything like the 2008 collapse from happening again. But that may be a vain hope or a case of wishful thinking. Experts in financial models have serious doubts about whether risk models can be improved in any fundamental way. What this means is as obvious as it is scary：banks and investment firms are leading the global economy into a future that is at great risk of repeating the past.

【譯文】：**一個經濟災難的公式**

將全球陷入經濟衰退並持續衰退的2008年市場暴跌有許多原因，其中一個原因是數學。金融投資公司發展出一些複雜的方式來投資客戶的金錢，而他們仰賴晦澀難解的公式來評估他們現有的風險。然而就像是我們3年前所學到的痛苦教訓，這些公式或是模型僅只是真實世界的蒼白反映；而令人遺憾的是，他們有時會誤導大家。

這正是風險模型被假設的力量賦予了投資公司信心，來對巨大的借款進行槓桿操作。這些模型會告訴他們這些賭注有多危險和哪些其他的投資可以抵銷那項風險。然而模型中巨大的不確定性給予了他們錯誤的信心。

因為這攸關成敗，在過去3年來金融公司已經投注了數以千萬美元來強化投資風險模型，並希望這些新的模型將可以杜絕類似於2008年的崩跌再度發生。但是這可能是一個空虛的希望或是一項一廂情願的想法。財金模型的專家們嚴重質疑風險模型能夠有根本上改善的想法。而這正意味著一樣不但明顯而且可怕的事情：銀行與投資公司正帶領著全球的經濟，陷入一個有巨大的風險，來重蹈過去覆轍的未來。

第一段：

文句1

【原文】：**A Formula for Economic Calamity**

The market crash of 2008 that plunged the world into the economic recession from which it is still reeling had many causes. One of them was mathematics.

【譯文】：一個經濟災難的公式

將全球陷入經濟衰退並持續衰退的2008年市場暴跌有許多原因，其中一個原因是數學。

【解析】：英譯中時，使用了Combining Skill（合併技巧），將英文原文的兩個句子翻譯為中文譯文的一個句子，使語意較為通順。

文句2

【原文】：Financial investment firms had developed such complex ways of investing their clients' money that they came to rely on arcane formulas to judge the risks they were taking on.

【譯文】：金融投資公司發展出一些複雜的方式來投資客戶的金錢，而他們仰賴晦澀難解的公式來評估他們現有的風險。

【解析】：英譯中時，使用了Splitting Skill（拆句技巧），將英文原文的 "that they came to rely on arcane formulas to judge the risks they were taking on"，在中文譯文中以「而他們仰賴晦澀難解的公式來評估他們現有的風險」翻譯之。

文句3

【原文】：Yet as we learned so **painfully** three years ago, those formulas, or models, are only pale reflections of the real world, and sometimes they can be woefully misleading.

【譯文】：然而就像是我們三年前學到的痛苦教訓，這些公式或是模型僅只是真實世界的蒼白反映；而令人遺憾的是，他們有時會誤導大家。

【解析】：英文原文中 "painfully" 是副詞，中文譯文中翻譯為「痛苦」，則為形容詞，這裡用到了Changing Skill（改變技巧）中的轉換詞性。

文句4

【原文】：woefully misleading

【譯文】：而令人遺憾的是

【解析】：英譯中時，將英文原文 "woefully" 這個副詞翻譯成中文譯文的「而令人遺憾的是」這個插入語，在翻譯技巧上是Changing Skill（改變技巧）。

第二段：

文句1

【原文】：It was **the supposed strength of risk models** that gave investment firms the confidence to leverage their bets with massive sums of borrowed money.

【譯文】：這正是風險模型被假設的力量賦予了投資公司信心，來對巨大的借款進行槓桿操作。

【解析】：（1）英譯中時，粗體字的部分使用了Changing Skill中的改變詞序。

（2）leverage [ˋlɛvərɪdʒ] 起槓桿作用；發揮重要功效

文句2

【原文】：The models would **tell them how risky these bets were** and what other investments would offset that risk.

【譯文】：這些模型會告訴他們這些賭注有多危險和哪些其他的投資可以抵銷那項風險。

【解析】：英譯中時，英文原文 "how risky these bets were" 轉換成中文譯文「這些賭注有多危險」，使用了Changing Skill中的改變詞序。

文句3

【原文】：Yet **the huge uncertainties in the models** gave them false confidence.

【譯文】：然而模型中巨大的不確定性給予了他們錯誤的信心。

【解析】：英文原文中，"uncertainties" 由兩個前位修飾 "the" 和 "huge"，及一個後位修飾 "in the models"；在中文譯文中，「不確定性」由兩個前位修飾「模型中」和「巨大的」來做修飾。這裡使用到了Changing Skill的改變詞序。

第三段：

文句1

【原文】：With so much at stake, in the past three years financial firms have spent tens of millions of dollars in buttressing their models of investment risk in the hope that new ones will preclude anything like the 2008 collapse from happening again.

【譯文】：因為這攸關成敗，在過去3年來金融公司已經投注了數以千萬美元來強化投資風險模型，並希望這些新的模型將可以杜絕類似2008年的崩跌再度發生。

【解析】：英譯中時，將英文原文的一句話翻譯為中文譯文的兩句話，使用了Splitting Skill（拆句技巧）。

文句2

【原文】：But that may be a vain hope or a case of wishful thinking.

【譯文】：但是這可能是一個空虛的希望或是一項一廂情願的想法。

【解析】：這句使用的方法是literal translation（直譯法），但是以符合中文習慣的句子來進行翻譯。

文句3

【原文】：experts in financial models

【譯文】：財金模型的專家們

【解析】：英譯中時，英文原文使用後位修飾，中文譯文使用前位修飾，是Changing Skill（改變技巧）的用法。

文句4

【原文】：have serious doubts

【譯文】：嚴重質疑

【解析】：英譯中時，英文原文使用了動詞加名詞的用法，中文譯文則彰顯出動詞「質疑」。

文句5

【原文】：What this means is as obvious as it is scary: banks and investment firms are leading the global economy into a future that is at great risk of repeating the past.

【譯文】：而這正意味著一樣不但明顯而且可怕的事情：銀行與投資公司正帶領著全球的經濟，陷入一個有巨大的風險，來重蹈過去覆轍的未來。

【解析】：在中文的譯文中使用了成語，「重蹈覆轍」來對應英文原文的 "repeating the past"，這個 "commonly used phrase"，算是做了有趣的對應。翻譯方法是 free translation（意譯法）。

中譯英一般文件筆譯類（一）

【原文】：**魔幻時刻**

　　親子關係就像是銀行的存摺一樣，最好把握各種機會，多貯存一些資產，留待孩子進入青春狂飆期或是長大離家產生疏離感之際使用。或許偶爾會有某個機緣、某個場景會留存在孩子的腦海中，一輩子陪伴著他們，當他們挫折困頓、憂傷沮喪，甚至感覺世界就要崩毀時，這些浮現腦海的記憶，可以適時地撫慰他們，成為支撐他們繼續前進的動力。像這種親子相處的美好回憶，可以稱為「魔幻時刻」。

　　有人覺得這些神奇的魔幻時刻是可遇而不可求的，或許真是如此，但父母至少可以營造某些情境與空間，透過刻意安排的活動，魔幻時刻比較容易出現。據我觀察，親子間輕鬆自在，沒有任何目的性地優游在大自然裡，不是為了學習什麼知識，也不是要應付學校的作業，只是單純享受微風吹過的感覺，蟲鳴鳥叫的天籟，親子之間深層的知心談心或許就會出現。另外，若全家能一起溯溪、攀岩，一起面對困境與挑戰，產生同心協力的感受，魔幻時刻也很容易在此時浮現。

【譯文】：**The Magic Moment**

　　Managing a parent-child relationship is just like possessing a bankbook. We had better grasp every opportunity and store as many assets as possible in order that we can use those assests when our children enter their adolescence or become alienated when growing up and going away from home. Maybe once in a while a moment or a scenario would remain in the children's minds, accompanying them throughout their lives. When they are frustrated, exhausted, sorrowful, or depressed, or when they feel the world would collapse, the memories surging from their minds can comfort them at the right moment and become the power which can support them to keep on. The fabulous memories shared by parents and children together could be termed as the "magic moment".

Some people may think that these miraculous magic moments are by chance and not by choice. Maybe it is true, but parents could at least try to create some scenarios and spaces. Through deliberately arranged activities, magic moments are more likely to occur. Based on my observation, deep and intimate talks between parents and children may occur when parents and children are carefree, aimlessly strolling in the nature, not to learn any knowledge or to cope with some assignments, but to simply enjoy the breezes blowing and the heavenly sounds of insects and birds choiring. In addition, the magic moments would be likely to appear at this moment when the family members go river trekking or rock climbing, face difficulties and challenges together, thus generating a feeling of teamwork.

第一段：

文句1

【原文】：親子關係就像是銀行的存摺一樣。

【譯文】：Managing a parent-child relationship is just like possessing a bankbook.

【解析】：（1）在中譯英時，爲了英文譯文的流暢性而加入了兩個動詞 "managing" 和 "possessing"，此時使用了Adding Approach（增加法）。

（2）存摺 a bankbook, a deposit book, a passbook, an account book

（3）挫折 a setback, a frustration, a discouragement

（4）困頓 tired out, exhausted, fatigued, weary, worn-out

（5）沮喪 depressed, dispirited, disheartened

（6）崩塌 to collapse, to crumble, to tumble down, to go to pieces

文句2

【原文】：這些浮現腦海的記憶

【譯文】：the memories surging from their minds

【解析】：（1）中文原文中採用前位修飾，英文譯文採用了後位修飾，在這裡用到了Changing Skill（改變技巧）。

（2）動力 power, motive power, motive force

文句3

【原文】：適時地撫慰他們

【譯文】：can comfort them at the right moment

【解析】：（1）在中文中，副詞的位置比較固定，大致都在所修飾動詞的前面，但是英文譯文中 "at the right moment" 則可以放在後面修飾 "comfort"，在這裡用到了 Changing Skill（改變技巧）。

（2）適時 timely, duly, at the right moment, in good time

文句4

【原文】：這種親子相處的美好回憶

【譯文】：The fabulous memories shared by parents and children together

【解析】：中文原文使用了三個前位修飾「這種」、「親子相處的」和「美好」來修飾「回憶」；在英文譯文中則使用了兩個前位修飾和一個後位修飾來修飾 "memories"，兩個前位修飾分別是 "The" 和 "fabulous"，後位修飾則是 "shared by parents and children together"，在這裡用到了Changing Skill（改變技巧）。

第二段：

文句1

【原文】：可遇而不可求的

【譯文】：by chance and not by choice

【解析】：中文原文「遇」和「求」皆爲動詞，在英文譯文中 "chance" 和 "choice" 則皆爲名詞，此處爲 Changing Skill（改變技巧）。

文句2

【原文】：另外，若全家能一起溯溪、攀岩，一起面對困境與挑戰，產生同心協力的感受，魔幻時刻也很容易在此時浮現。

【譯文】：In addition, the magic moments would be likely to appear at this moment when the family go river trekking or rock climbing, face difficulties and challenges together, thus generating a feeling of teamwork.

【解析】：中文原文中，副詞子句「若全家能一起溯溪、攀岩，一起面對困境與挑戰，產生同心協力的感受」放在主要子句「魔幻時刻也很容易在此時浮現」的前面；在英文譯文中主要子句 "the magic moments would be likely to appear" 放在前面，副詞子句 "face difficulties and challenges together, thus generating a feeling of teamwork" 則放在後面。這裡使用的翻譯手法是Restructuring Skill（重組技巧）。

中譯英一般文件筆譯類（二）

【原文】：**節食能減重嗎？**

減重之所以不容易成功，牽涉到身體本能的求生原則，和懶惰與否、意志堅定與否關聯不大。當你用粗魯、不符合本性的方式減重時，身體會自然產生反抗，你也不可能會感到快樂。

節食減重就像和上帝拔河一樣，毫無勝算。或許你會覺得奇怪，既然肥胖是因為攝取過多熱量，那麼節食為什麼不是減重的基本原則？積極節食與身體本能間，是否會相互抵觸？

積極節食其實就是告訴身體「饑荒來了」。這時，身體會自動啟動下列幾種功能：一、提高身體飢餓感；二、降低基礎代謝率，減少每日消耗熱量；三、攝取食物後，將熱量完全吸收。

所以，最有效的減重方式，就是不要讓自己感到過度飢餓。「飢餓」是一種降低身體代謝率的訊號，時常發出這種訊號，只會增加減重的難度。想要順利減重，請務必記得：不要讓自己處在非常飢餓的狀態、每日攝取的熱量絕對不能低於1000大卡、每隔4至5小時就該補充符合自己代謝型態的食物，避免等到過度飢餓才吃。

【譯文】：**Can Going on a Diet Help Lose Your Weight?**

Why it is not an easy task to be successful with weight loss is related to the survival principle of body instinct, which has little to do with whether someone is lazy or determined. When you lose your weight in a way which is rude and does not correspond to your nature, your body will naturally respond to it with resistance, and there is no way you can feel happy.

Going on a diet to lose weight is like playing a tug-of-war with God; you just do not stand a chance of success. Maybe you will feel it is odd. Since obesity results in excessive intake of calories, why is dieting not the basic principle of losing weight? Does active weight loss and body instinct conflict with each other?

Active dieting is actually telling the body, "here comes the famine." In this case, the body will automatically start the following functions: first, to enhance the sense of physical hunger; second, to reduce the basic metabolic rate so as to decrease your daily calorie consumption; and third, to completely absorb the calories after the food intake.

Therefore, the most effective way to lose weight is not to let yourself feel excessively hungry. "Hunger" is a signal to reduce the body's metabolic rate; if these signals are often sent out, it will only increase the difficulty of losing weight. To successfully lose weight, be sure to remember: do not keep yourself in a very hungry state; daily intake of calories must not be less than one thousand calories; supplement food in line with your own metabolic patterns every four to five hours, and avoid eating only after the moment when you feel excessively hungry.

第一段：

文句1

【原文】：減重之所以不容易成功，牽涉到身體本能的求生原則

【譯文】：Why it is not an easy task to be successful with weight loss is related to the survival principle of body instinct

【解析】：（1）英文譯文使用了 "why" 所引導的名詞子句，所以將中文的兩句話合併為英文的一句話，使用了Combining Skill（合併技巧）。

（2）節食 to be on a weight-losing diet, to diet, to go on a diet

文句2

【原文】：當你用粗魯、不符合本性的方式減重時，身體會自然產生反抗，你也不可能會感到快樂。

【譯文1】：When you lose your weight **in a way which is rude and does not correspond to** your nature, your body will naturally respond to it with resistance, and there is no way you can feel happy.

【譯文2】：When you lose your weight **in a way which is rude and is at odds with** your nature, your body will naturally respond to it with resistance, and there is no way you can feel happy.

【解析】：（1）中文原文的「方式」使用了兩個前位修飾，分別是「粗魯」和「不符合本性」；英文譯文的 "way" 則使用了一個前位修飾 "a" 和一個後位修飾方式，形容詞子句 "which is rude and does not correspond to your nature"。

（2）與……不一致 be at odds with...

第二段：

文句1

【原文】：節食減重就像和上帝拔河一樣，毫無勝算。

【譯文1】：Going on a diet to lose weight is like playing a tug-of-war with God; you just do not stand a chance of success.

【解析】：中文原文中只有一句話，而英文譯文中因為英文是形合的語言及注重主詞突顯，因此需要有兩個主詞而產生了兩句的英文譯文。這個地方採用了Splitting Skill（拆句技巧）。

【譯文2】：Going on a diet to lose weight is like playing a tug-of-war with God; you just do not stand a chance of success.

【解析】：英文譯文增加了 "you"，採用了Adding Approach（增加法）。

文句2

【原文】：或許你會覺得奇怪，**既然**肥胖是因為攝取過多熱量，**那麼**節食為什麼不是減重的基本原則？

【譯文】：Maybe you will feel it is odd. Since obesity results in excessive intake of calories, why is dieting not the basic principle of losing weight?

【解析】：（1）中文的句法允許每一個子句都有連接詞連接，像是中文原文的「既然」及「那麼」這兩個連接詞，但是在英文的從屬關係中，連接詞只能夠出現在附屬子句的前面，即如上面的 "since"。這裡使用到了翻譯方法中的 Changing Skill（改變技巧）。

（2）奇怪 odd, queer, strange, surprising, unusual, funny, pe-culiar, frea-kish

文句3

【原文】：積極節食與身體本能間，是否會相互抵觸？

【譯文】：Does active weight loss and body instinct conflict with each other?

【解析】：這裡使用的是直譯（literal translation）。

第三段：

【原文】：積極節食其實就是告訴身體「饑荒來了」。這時，身體會自動啟動下列幾種功能：一、提高身體飢餓感；二、降低基礎代謝率，減少每日消耗熱量；三、攝取食物後，將熱量完全吸收。

【譯文】：Active dieting is actually telling the body, "here comes the famine." In this case, the body will automatically start the following functions: first, to enhance the sense of physical hunger; second, to reduce the basic metabolic rate so as to decrease your daily calorie consumption; **and** third, to completely absort the calories after the food intake.

【解析】：（1）這裡使用的是直譯（literal translation）。

（2）攝取食物 food intake, ingestion of food

（3）"third" 之前需加上 "and"。

第四段：

文句1

【原文】：所以，最有效的減重方式，就是不要讓自己感到過度飢餓。

【譯文】：Therefore, the most effective way to lose weight is not to let yourself feel excessively hungry.

【解析】：中文原文減重方式是前位修飾，英文譯文 "way to lose weight" 是後位修飾。這裡使用的翻譯方法是Changing Skill中的改變詞序。

文句2

【原文】：想要順利減重，請務必記得：不要讓自己處在非常飢餓的狀態、每日攝取的熱量絕對不能低於1000大卡、每隔4至5小時就該補充符合自己代謝型態的食物、避免等到過度飢餓才吃。

【譯文】：**To successfully lose weight**, be sure to remember: do not keep yourself in a very hungry state; daily intake of calories must not be less than one thousand calories; supplement food in line with your own metabolic patterns every four to five hours, and avoid eating only after the moment when you feel excessively hungry.

【解析】：在中文原文中的「想要順利減重」可以用 "To successfully lose weight" 這樣子的不定詞片語來做翻譯，其中的不定詞突顯了「想要」的這個概念。這裡使用的翻譯方法是 Changing Skill（改變技巧）。

99 年教育部中英文翻譯能力檢定考試試題

英譯中一般文件筆譯類

【原文】：**Unpluggable**

　　Secrets are as old as states, and so are enemies', critics' and busybodies' efforts to uncover them. But the impact and scale of the latest disclosures by WikiLeaks, a secretive and autocratic website that campaigns for openness, are on a new level. A disillusioned 23-year-old American official downloaded from a supposedly secure government network more than 250,000 diplomatic "cables"：in effect, government e-mails. He gave the cables to WikiLeaks, which in turn provided them to international news outlets.

　　The first slivers appearing in late November range from the explosive to the inconsequential. Diplomats being instructed to act like spies, snooping on the UN Secretary General and filching the frequent-flyer and credit-card details of other senior UN officials, sounds like a scandal. But solemnly recording that the Russian prime minister is the real power in his country, or that the Italian leader enjoys hard partying, or that the French president is vain and mercurial, seems a waste of taxpayers' electrons.

For the most part, the leaks' content is less important than their source, and the manner of the betrayal. Individually, the disclosures are trivial：some would be barely newsworthy if published legally. But collectively, they are corrosive. America appears humiliatingly unable to keep its own or other people's secrets.

It would be an exaggeration to say that diplomacy will never be the same. Self-interest means countries will still exchange private messages. But communication will be more difficult. The trading of intelligence and favours necessarily requires shadow, not light. Unofficial contacts such as businessmen, journalists and other citizens who talk to American diplomats will think twice about doing so.

【譯文】：**維基解密，人人自危**

隨著國家成立時間的長遠，祕密就伴隨著有多少，而敵方、評論家、好事之徒對於揭密之心力，亦同如此。最近維基解密網站爆料了一些事情，其衝擊與規模達到了新的程度。維基解密係一為了爭取公開而積極活動祕密與專制的網站。一位23歲幻想破滅的美國官員，從一個據稱是安全的政府網站，下載了多達25萬多筆的外交「電訊」，實際上也就是政府的「電子郵件」。這些「電訊」後來交給了維基解密，而後將之提供給國際新聞媒體。

去年11月下旬出現的第一批解密資料，範圍涉及爆發性的資料與無關緊要的資料。外交官曾窺探聯合國祕書長，一手竊取了其他資深聯合國官員的飛行常客與信用卡明細表，而外交官被指示像間諜一樣的行為，聽起來像是一個醜聞。至於其他正式的紀錄資料似乎是浪費了納稅人錢的無謂電報，例如：蘇俄首相握有國家實權，義大利領導人喜好尋歡作樂，法國總統虛榮善變。

整體來說，消息來源與洩密方式比維基解密的內容重要。以個人而言，真相的揭發其實無關緊要，就算是合法公布，有一些揭發的事情也幾乎沒有任何新聞價值。但是以全體而言，卻是有侵蝕性的。美國很羞愧，它似乎無法保守其自己或其他人民的祕密。

若說外交手腕永遠不會一樣，算是浮誇之詞。為了自身利益，國與國之間會互相交換非公開的訊息，但是溝通會更困難。情報與小禮物的交易必然見不得陽光。非官方的接觸，例如：商人、新聞記者，或是其他平民，如果和美國外交官談話，最好還是三思而後行。

第一段：

【原文】：**Unpluggable**

Secrets are as old as states, and so are enemies', critics' and busybodies' efforts to uncover them. But the impact and scale of the latest disclosures by WikiLeaks, a secretive and autocratic website that campaigns for openness, are on a new level. A disillusioned 23-year-old American official downloaded from a supposedly secure government network more than 250,000 diplomatic "cables"：in effect, government e-mails. He gave the cables to WikiLeaks, which in turn provided them to international news outlets.

【譯文】：**維基解密，人人自危**

隨著國家成立時間的長遠，祕密就伴隨著有多少，而敵方、評論家、好事之徒對於揭密之心力，亦同如此。最近維基解密網站爆料了一些事情，其衝擊與規模達到了新的程度。維基解密係一為了爭取公開而積極活動祕密與專制的網站。一位23歲幻想破滅的美國官員，從一個據稱是安全的政府網站，下載了多達25萬多筆的外交「電訊」，實際上也就是政府的「電子郵件」。這些「電訊」後來交給了維基解密，而後將之提供給國際新聞媒體。

【解析】：（1）拆句與重組：But the impact and scale of the latest disclosures by WikiLeaks, a secretive and autocratic website that campaigns for openness, are on a new level. 最近維基解密網站爆料了一些事情，其衝擊與規模達到了新的程度。維基解密係一為了爭取公開而積極活動祕密與專制的網站。

（2）disclosure [dɪsˋkloʒɚ] 揭發；透露；公開；揭發（或敗露）的事情

（3）disillusioned [ˏdɪsɪˋluʒənd] 不抱幻想的；幻想破滅的

（4）supposedly [səˋpozɪdlɪ] 根據推測；據稱；大概，可能

（5）in effect 在功效方面；實際上

（6）in turn 按順序；依次

（7）轉譯："outlet"「銷路；商店，商行」轉譯為「媒體」。

第二段：

【原文】：The first slivers appearing in late November range from the explosive to the inconsequential. Diplomats being instructed to act like spies, snooping on the UN Secretary General and

filching the frequent-flyer and credit-card details of other senior UN officials, sounds like a scandal. But solemnly recording that the Russian prime minister is the real power in his
country, or that the Italian leader enjoys hard partying, or that
the French president is vain and mercurial, seems a waste of
taxpayers' electrons.

【譯文】：去年11月下旬出現的第一批解密資料，範圍涉及爆發性的
資料與無關緊要的資料。外交官曾窺探聯合國祕書長，一
手竊取了其他資深聯合國官員的飛行常客與信用卡明細
表，而外交官被指示像間諜一樣的行為，聽起來像是一個
醜聞。至於其他正式的紀錄資料似乎是浪費了納稅人錢的
無謂電報，例如：蘇俄首相握有國家實權，義大利領導人
喜好尋歡作樂，法國總統虛榮善變。

【解析】：（1）sliver [`slɪvɚ] 裂片

（2）explosive [ɪk`splosɪv] 爆炸（性）的；爆發性的

（3）inconsequential [ˌɪnkɑnsə`kwɛnʃəl] 無關緊要的；不重
要的

（4）snoop [snup] 窺探

（5）filch [fɪltʃ] 偷（少量或不貴重的東西）

（6）scandal [`skændl̩] 醜聞，醜事

（7）hard partying 尋歡作樂

（8）mercurial [mɝ`kjʊrɪəl]（情緒）易變的；反覆無常的

（9）重組：The first slivers appearing in late November
range from the explosive to the inconsequential. 去年11
月下旬出現的第一批解密資料，範圍涉及爆發性的
資料與無關緊要的資料。

191

第三段：

【原文】：For the most part, the leaks' content is less important than their source, and the manner of the betrayal. Individually, the disclosures are trivial：some would be barely newsworthy if published legally. But collectively, they are corrosive. America appears humiliatingly unable to keep its own or other people's secrets.

【譯文】：整體來說，消息來源與洩密方式比維基解密的內容重要。以個人而言，真相的揭發其實無關緊要，就算是合法公布，有一些揭發的事情也幾乎沒有任何新聞價值。但是以全體而言，卻是有侵蝕性的。美國很羞愧，它似乎無法保守其自己或其他人民的祕密。

【解析】：（1）for the most part 大多數情況下；主要地；整體上；通常；多半

（2）轉譯："the leaks' content is less important than their source, and the manner of the betrayal" 轉譯為「消息來源與洩密方式比維基解密的內容重要」。

（3）corrosive [kə`rosɪv] 腐蝕的；侵蝕性的

（4）humiliatingly [hju`mɪlɪˏetɪŋlɪ] 丟臉地；恥辱地；羞愧地

（5）重組：America appears humiliatingly unable to keep its own or other people's secrets. 美國很羞愧，它似乎無法保守其自己的人民或其他人民的祕密。

第四段：

【原文】：It would be an exaggeration to say that diplomacy will never be the same. Self-interest means countries will still exchange private messages. But communication will be more difficult.

The trading of intelligence and favours necessarily requires shadow, not light. Unofficial contacts such as businessmen, journalists and other citizens who talk to American diplomats will think twice about doing so.

【譯文】：若說外交手腕永遠不會一樣，算是浮誇之詞。爲了自身利益，國與國之間會互相交換非公開的訊息，但是溝通會更困難。情報與小禮物的交易必然見不得陽光。非官方的接觸，例如：商人、新聞記者，或是其他平民，如果和美國外交官談話，最好還是三思而後行。

【解析】：（1）diplomacy [dɪˋploməsɪ] 外交手腕

（2）轉譯與合併：Self-interest means countries will still exchange private messages. But communication will be more difficult. 爲了自身利益，國與國之間會互相交換非公開的訊息，但是溝通會更困難。

中譯英一般文件筆譯類（一）

【原文】：**魔術與科學都從神祕開始**

對許多華人而言，講到魔術師，從前想到的是曾把自由女神像變不見的美國魔術師考伯菲，現在腦中浮現的名字則是劉謙。

12歲那年劉謙參加一項臺灣青少年魔術競賽，由考伯菲手中拿下最大獎。如今34歲的他，已是國際魔術界最高榮譽梅林獎「世界魔術傑出貢獻獎」得主，不但連續2年受邀在北京的春節晚會表演，更是第一位踏上美國拉斯維加斯、好萊塢，在魔術表演聖地「魔術城堡」演出的華人魔術師。

科學的奧妙與魔術的奇幻曾同時吸引著劉謙，但因為特別喜愛「表演」，所以走上了職業魔術師的路。他從小愛看科普書、喜歡胡思亂想。身為家中獨生子，為了自得其樂，經常照著書上的內容細細研究實驗。又因為自尊心強，所以決定成為魔術師後，除了心理學、理化、光學、色彩學等魔術專業，還拚了命的念語文、出國比賽、做國際交流。

　　劉謙最近一直在思考的魔術，是如何從薄薄的液晶電視裡，毫無遮掩的直接爬出來。「從來沒人做過，我已經想了兩年了。」劉謙笑著說：「如果成功，效果應該會非常震撼吧。」

　　詞彙：考伯菲 David Copperfield

　　　　　劉謙 Lu Chen

　　　　　梅林獎 Merlin Awards

　　　　　世界魔術傑出貢獻獎 Outstanding Contribution
　　　　　　　　　　　　　　　　to World Magic Award

　　　　　拉斯維加斯 Las Vegas

　　　　　好萊塢 Hollywood

【譯文】：**Both Magic and Science Begin with Mystery**

　　For many ethnic Chinese, when it comes to magicians, they used to think of the American magician David Copperfield, who once made the Statue of Liberty invisible, but now the name of Lu Chen comes to their minds instead.

　　At the age of 12, Lu Chen participated in an Adolescent Magic Competition in Taiwan, and won the biggest award from the hands of David Copperfield. Now at the age of 34, he was the winner of the highest honor in the international magic field, the Merlin Awards, "Outstanding Contribution to World Magic Award". He not only accepted invitations to perform magic for two consecutive years in Beijing New Year's Gala, but was also the first ethnic Chinese magician that set foot on American Las Vegas and Hollywood, performing magic at the holy ground of magic performance, "The Magic Castle".

Both the wonder of science and the fantasy of magic attracted Lu Chen simultaneously. But since he was particularly fond of "performance", Lu decided to embark on the career as a professional magician. Ever since he was a little boy, he has enjoyed reading popular science books and going off into wild flights of fancy. As the only son of the family, he often carefully studied and conducted experiments following the contents of the books so as to enjoy delights in his own way. After having decided to become a magician, with high self-esteem, he also put in a great deal of effort to study language, participate in international competitions, and interact with magicians from other countries, aside from other magic expertise such as psychology, physical chemistry, optics, and chromotology.

The magic that Lu Chen has been thinking about recently is how to undisguisedly directly climb out of the thin liquid crystal display (LCD) television. "No one has ever done this before, and I have been thinking about it for two years," Lu Chen said with a smile, "If it turns out successful, the effect should be breathtaking."

第一段：

【原文】：對許多華人而言，**講到魔術師**，從前想到的是曾把自由女神像變不見的美國魔術師考伯菲，現在腦中浮現的名字則是劉謙。

【譯文】：For many ethnic Chinese, **when it comes to magicians**, they used to think of the American magician David Copperfield, who once made the Statue of Liberty invisible, but now the name of Lu Chen comes to their minds instead.

【解析】：中文原文中插入語「講到魔術師」隱含了時間的概念，但是因為中文是意合的語言，所以不必言明。但是在英文譯文中的插入語 "when it comes to magicians" 就較有言明 "when" 這個有時間意味的連接詞的必要，因為英文是形合的語言，較重視結構的完整性。

此處採用的翻譯方法是Adding Approach（增加法）。

第二段：

文句1

【原文】：12歲那年劉謙參加一項臺灣青少年魔術競賽，由考伯菲手中拿下最大獎。

【譯文】：At the age of 12, Lu Chen participated in an Adolescent Magic Competition in Taiwan, and won the biggest award from the hands of David Copperfield.

【解析】：這裡使用的是直譯（literal translation）。

文句2

【原文】：如今34歲的他，已是國際魔術界最高榮譽梅林獎「世界魔術傑出貢獻獎」得主，不但連續2年受邀在北京的春節晚會表演，更是第一位踏上美國拉斯維加斯、好萊塢，在魔術表演聖地「魔術城堡」演出的華人魔術師。

【譯文】：Now at the age of 34, **he** was the winner of the highest honor in the international magic field, the Merlin Awards, "Outstanding Contribution to World Magic Award". He not only accepted invitations to perform magic for two consecutive years in

實用中英翻譯法

Beijing New Year's Gala, but was also the first ethnic Chinese magician that set foot on American Las Vegas and Hollywood, and performing magic at the holy ground of magic performance, "The Magic Castle".

【解析】：改變了中文原文和英文譯文主詞的位置，使用了翻譯方法中的 Restructuring Skill（重組技巧）。

　　第三段：

　　文句1

【原文】：科學的奧妙與魔術的奇幻曾同時吸引著劉謙，但因為特別喜愛「表演」，所以走上了職業魔術師的路。

【譯文】：Both the wonder of science and the fantasy of magic attracted Lu Chen simultaneously. But since he was particularly fond of "performance", Lu decided to embark on the career as a professional magician.

【解析】：中文原文中一個長句裡的數個短句中的主詞可以不相同，而且各短句不需要用連接詞連接，甚至主詞也可以做省略，因為中文是一個主題優先的語言。但是英文是一個主詞優先的語言，所以各個短句中的主詞必須彰顯，而各短句需要有連接詞做連接。如同英文譯文中第一句的主詞是 "the wonder of science and the fantasy of magic"，第二句的主詞是 "Lu"，這兩個英文句子因為主詞不同，在這裡就需要以句點分開。

　　這裡使用的翻譯方法是 Changing Skill（改變技巧）和 Splitting Skill（拆句技巧）。

　　文句2

【原文】：他從小愛看科普書、喜歡胡思亂想。

【譯文1】：**Ever since he was a little boy**, he has enjoyed reading popular science books and going off into wild flights of fancy.

【譯文2】：He has enjoyed reading popular science books and going off into wild flights of fancy **ever since he was a little boy**.

【解析】：（1）中文原文中的「從小」通常需要放在靠近主詞的地方，而英文譯文中的 "since he was a little boy" 位置則相對自由。此處採用的翻譯方法是Changing Skill（改變技巧）。

（2）胡思亂想 to go off into wild flights of fancy, to have idle fancy, to have wild flights of fancy

文句3

【原文】：身為家中獨生子，為了自得其樂，經常照著書上的內容細細研究實驗。又因為自尊心強，所以決定成為魔術師後，除了心理學、理化、光學、色彩學等魔術專業，還拚了命的念語文、出國比賽、做國際交流。

【譯文】：As the only son of the family, he often carefully studied and conducted experiments following the contents of the books so as to enjoy delights in his own way. After having decided to become a magician, with high self-esteem, he also put in a great deal of effort to study language, participate in international competitions, and interact with magicians from other countries, aside from other magic expertise such as psychology, physical chemistry, optics, and chromotology.

【解析】：這裡使用的是直譯（literal translation）。

第四段：

文句1

【原文】：劉謙最近一直在思考的魔術

【譯文】：The magic that Lu Chen has been thinking about recently

【解析】：中文原文中「魔術」有一個前位修飾「劉謙最近一直在思考的」，英文譯文則有一個前位修飾"The"，和一個後位修飾"that Lu Chen has been thinking about recently"。此處使用到的翻譯方法是Restructuring Skill（重組技巧）。

文句2

【原文】：劉謙最近一直在思考的魔術，是如何從薄薄的液晶電視裡，毫無遮掩的直接爬出來。

【譯文】：The magic that Lu Chen has been thinking about recently is how to undisguisedly directly climb out of the thin liquid crystal display (LCD) television.

【解析】：英文譯文中使用了名詞片語 "how to undisguisedly directly climb out of the thin liquid crystal display (LCD) television"，精簡了句子的數量。此處使用了Combining Skill（合併技巧）。

文句3

【原文】：「從來沒人做過，我已經想了兩年了。」劉謙笑著說：「如果成功，效果應該會非常震撼吧。」

【譯文】："No one has ever done this before, and I have been thinking about it for two years," Lu Chen said with a smile, "If it turns out successful, the effect should be breathtaking."

【解析】：中文原文「笑著說」，英文譯文則翻譯為 "said with a smile"，同時使用到了 Changing Skill 的改變詞序（中文「笑」在「說」前面，英文譯文 "said" 在 "smile" 前面）和 Changing Skill 的改變詞性（中文原文「笑」是動詞而英文譯文 "smile" 是名詞）。

98 年教育部中英文翻譯能力檢定考試試題

英譯中一般文件筆譯類（一）

【原文】：**Who Knows Best?**

Wikipedia, the web-based, collaborative encyclopedia launched in 2001 by a few people with very big scrapbooks and maybe a little too much time on their hands, is under threat.

The online site—the name derives from a combination of the Hawaiian word wiki, meaning "quick", and pedia, the Latin for "feet", denoting a surfer's ability to sprint through reams of information very rapidly—is suffering from an exodus of the volunteer editors who write, fact-check and edit Wikipedia entries.

Given that Wikipedia relies on such editors to keep its entries fresh, relevant and accurate, it is feared that this drain threatens the site's future. Because once Wikipedia loses its reputation for up-to-date reliability, users may migrate elsewhere when they next need suddenly to pretend to their boss or their tutor that they are deeply knowledgeable about the Chinese bond market, or the Battle of Naseby.

The volunteer editors are complaining of a rise in Kafkaesque bureaucracy and rules—introduced to stifle rogue incidents of misinformation being planted in Wikipedia articles. It is an interference that they consider to be alien to the spirit of a "wisdom of crowds" website. Editors are also bridling at pages on controversial subjects, such as the Holocaust or Islam, being locked to prevent their being edited.

As a result, Wikipedia is facing a choice：to grow very fast until no subject is left uncovered, however trifling; or to impose editing restrictions that burnish its standing as a trustworthy reference source. It's the one question to which the Wikipedia site provides no answers.

【譯文】：誰最了解？

一群人於2001年推出以網頁爲基礎、互助式的百科全書維基百科，而這花了不少時間及需要大量的剪貼簿所建置的維基百科正面臨威脅。

維基百科這個名稱是源於兩個字的組合，它是由"wiki"及"pedia"所組成，"wiki"是夏威夷文，指的是「快速」的意思，而"pedia"在拉丁文中有「腳」之意，結合起來即表示一個衝浪手在大量的資訊中快速穿梭的能力。然而這網站正受到志願編輯者離開的危機，這些編輯者負責維基百科的詞條撰寫、求證及編輯。

考慮到維基百科得依賴這些編輯者，以保持資訊新穎、高相關性及高準確度，恐怕這不斷外流的情況會威脅維基百科的未來。原因在於一旦維基百科失去最新的可靠性之名聲，當使用者突然需要對老闆或輔導教師假裝他們對中國債券市場或內斯比之戰有很豐富的知識，他們則會轉向使用其他網站資料。

對於卡夫卡式的繁文縟節與規範的興盛，志願編輯者皆有所抱怨——阻止不可靠的資訊植入於維基百科的文章中。維基百科網站是以「群眾的智慧」的精神爲本，這些編輯群認爲它是個干擾，與「群眾的智慧」的精神不相容。編輯者們也對於無法編撰具爭議性的議題氣惱，像是大屠殺或是回教等議題。

而結果就是維基百科正面臨一個抉擇：快速發展直到

沒有更新的題材，然而這微不足道。抑或是強加編輯的限制規定，提升其名望，成為可靠的參考資料來源。這是一個維基百科網站無法提供答案的問題。

第一段：

【原文】：**Who Knows Best?**

Wikipedia, the web-based, collaborative encyclopedia launched in 2001 by a few people with very big scrapbooks and maybe a little too much time on their hands, is under threat.

【譯文】：**誰最了解？**

一群人於2001年推出以網頁為基礎、互助式的百科全書維基百科，而這花了不少時間及需要大量的剪貼簿所建置的維基百科正面臨威脅。

【解析】：重組：Wikipedia is under threat。

第二段：

【原文】：The online site－the name derives from a combination of the Hawaiian word wiki, meaning "quick", and pedia, the Latin for "feet", denoting a surfer's ability to sprint through reams of information very rapidly－is suffering from an exodus of the volunteer editors who write, fact-check and edit Wikipedia entries.

【譯文】：維基百科這個名稱是源於兩個字的組合，它是由 "wiki" 及 "pedia" 所組成，"wiki" 是夏威夷文，指的是「快速」的意思，而 "pedia" 在拉丁文中有「腳」之意，結合起來即表示一個衝浪手在大量的資訊中快速穿梭的能力。然而這網站正受到志願編輯者離開的危機，這些編輯者負責維基百科的詞條撰寫、求證及編輯。

【解析】：（1）重組：The online site is suffering from an exodus of the volunteer editors who write, fact-check and edit Wikipedia entries.

（2）exodus [ˋɛksədəs] 外出；離開

（3）suffer from... 遭受……之苦；遭受……之困擾；遭受……之危機

第三段：

【原文】：Given that Wikipedia relies on such editors to keep its entries fresh, relevant and accurate, it is feared that this drain threatens the site's future. Because once Wikipedia loses its reputation for up-to-date reliability, users may migrate elsewhere when they next need suddenly to pretend to their boss or their tutor that they are deeply knowledgeable about the Chinese bond market, or the Battle of Naseby.

【譯文】：考慮到維基百科得依賴這些編輯者，以保持資訊新穎、高相關性及高準確度，恐怕這不斷外流的情況會威脅維基百科的未來。原因在於一旦維基百科失去最新的可靠性之名聲，當使用者突然需要對老闆或輔導教師假裝他們對中國債券市場或內斯比之戰有很豐富的知識，他們則會轉向使用其他網站資料。

【解析】：（1）given + N. 如果有；假如

　　　　　given that 考慮到

（2）增譯：「高相關性」及「高準確度」。

（3）轉譯："users may migrate elsewhere" 轉譯為「他們則會轉向使用其他網站資料」。

203

第四段：

【原文】：The volunteer editors are complaining of a rise in Kafkaesque bureaucracy and rules－introduced to stifle rogue incidents of misinformation being planted in Wikipedia articles. It is an interference that they consider to be alien to the spirit of a "wisdom of crowds" website. Editors are also bridling at pages on controversial subjects, such as the Holocaust or Islam, being locked to prevent their being edited.

【譯文】：對於卡夫卡式的繁文縟節與規範的興盛，志願編輯者皆有所抱怨──阻止不可靠的資訊植入於維基百科的文章中。維基百科網站是以「群衆的智慧」的精神爲本，這些編輯群認爲它是個干擾，與「群衆的智慧」的精神不相容。編輯者們也對於無法編撰具爭議性的議題氣惱，像是大屠殺或是回教等議題。

【解析】：（1）stifle [`staɪfl] 抑止；阻止

（2）rogue incidents 不可靠事件

（3）alien 性質不同的；不相容的；格格不入[(+to)]

（4）bridel [`braɪdl] 動怒，生氣[(+at)]

（5）重組：Editors are also bridling at pages on controversial subjects, such as the Holocaust or Islam, being locked to prevent their being edited. 編輯者們也對於無法編撰具爭議性的議題氣惱，像是大屠殺或是回教等議題。

第五段：

【原文】：As a result, Wikipedia is facing a choice：to grow very fast until no subject is left uncovered, however trifling; or to impose editing restrictions that burnish its standing as a trust-

實用中英翻譯法

worthy reference source. It's the one question to which the Wikipedia site provides no answers.

【譯文】：而結果就是維基百科正面臨一個抉擇：快速發展直到沒有更新的題材，然而這微不足道。抑或是強加編輯的限制規定，提升其名望，成爲可靠的參考資料來源。這是一個維基百科網站無法提供答案的問題。

【解析】：（1）trifling [ˋtraɪflɪŋ] 不重要的；微不足道的

（2）burnish [ˋbɝnɪʃ] 擦亮；使光亮；磨光

（3）standing 地位；名望

（4）轉譯：burnish its standing 提升其名望。

英譯中一般文件筆譯類（二）

【原文】：**A Ban on Genetic Discrimination**

It is rare when antidiscrimination law is extended to a whole new group of people, but that happened on Saturday, when a US federal ban on discriminating on the basis of genetic background took effect. The new law is an important step in protecting people who have inherited a predisposition to disease. It removes a significant obstacle to genetic testing, which can warn people that they have a disposition for diseases like cancer, and can help doctors adapt courses of treatment to particular patients.

As advances have been made in genetic testing, however, employers and insurance companies have used it to penalize people. There have been reports of people being denied jobs or being fired because a parent had Huntington's disease, or the worker had a BRCA1 gene that predisposed her to breast and ovarian cancer. People with family histories of certain diseases have had difficulty in buying health insurance.

The Genetic Information Nondiscrimination Act ushers in a new era. The law prohibits employers from asking for genetic tests or taking into account an employee's genetic background in hiring, firing or promotions. It prohibits discrimination on the basis of genetic background in group and individual health insurance plans.

Some insurance companies and business groups opposed the law, arguing that it was unfair and unnecessarily burdensome. But the Senate passed it unanimously, and the House with only one "no" vote, because lawmakers rightly saw that fairness and public policy arguments demanded a ban on discriminating against people for genetic traits they can do nothing about.

【譯文】：**禁止基因歧視**

反歧視法延伸到全新族群的現象極為罕見，而此現象就在週六發生。一項美國聯邦法令生效，該法令是禁止對基因背景的歧視。這項新法令能保護帶有先天疾病傾向的民眾，是一個重要的步驟。這法令移除了基因測試的重大障礙，基因測試可以警告人們他們帶有像是癌症的傾向，並幫助醫生對特殊的患者採取治療方向。

基因測試已經有發展，然而，雇主與保險公司卻利用這點來處罰人們。已有幾個報導是有關於民眾無法獲得工作或被解僱，只因為他／她的父親或母親有杭廷頓舞蹈症，或是員工被診斷出帶有BRCA1基因，使她容易得到乳癌或是卵巢癌，而受到不平等待遇。帶有家族某些疾病歷史的民眾要買健康保險也不是那麼容易。

基因資訊反歧視法案開創了一個新世代。該法案禁止雇主要求雇員做基因測試，也禁止雇主在徵人、解僱、升遷時，將員工基因背景納入考量。有關群體或個人的健保計畫，此法案防止基於基因背景這方面的歧視。

　　有一些保險公司和商業團體反對這項法案，他們認為這法案沒有公平性可言，而且根本沒有存在的必要，反而造成諸多困擾。然而參議院一致通過這項法案，眾議院也只有一個反對票，因為立法者公正地理解這項法案的公平性，而且諸多公共政策議題要求一個針對這類歧視的法令，來幫助帶有基因特徵卻無計可施的人。

　第一段：

【原文】：**A Ban on Genetic Discrimination**

　　It is rare when antidiscrimination law is extended to a whole new group of people, but that happened on Saturday, when a US federal ban on discriminating on the basis of genetic background took effect. The new law is an important step in protecting people who have inherited a predisposition to disease. It removes a significant obstacle to genetic testing, which can warn people that they have a disposition for diseases like cancer, and can help doctors adapt courses of treatment to particular patients.

【譯文】：禁止基因歧視

　　反歧視法延伸到全新族群的現象極為罕見，而此現象就在週六發生。一項美國聯邦法令生效，該法令是禁止對基因背景的歧視。這項新法令能保護帶有先天疾病傾向的民眾，是一個重要的步驟。這法令移除了基因測試的重大障礙，基因測試可以警告人們他們帶有像是癌症的傾向，並幫助醫生對特殊的患者採取治療方向。

【解析】：（1）主被動轉譯：It is rare when antidiscrimination law is extended to a whole new group of people. 反歧視法延伸到全新族群的現象極為罕見。

（2）重組：It is rare when antidiscrimination law is extended to a whole new group of people. 反歧視法延伸到全新族群的現象極為罕見。

（3）拆句：but that happened on Saturday, when a US federal ban on discriminating on the basis of genetic background took effect. 而此現象就在週六發生。一項美國聯邦法令生效，該法令是禁止對基因背景的歧視。

（4）重組：The new law is an important step in protecting people who have inherited a predisposition to disease. 這項新法令能保護帶有先天疾病的民眾，是一個重要的步驟。

（5）disposistion to... 有……的傾向

第二段：

【原文】：As advances have been made in genetic testing, however, employers and insurance companies have used it to penalize people. There have been reports of people being denied jobs or being fired because a parent had Huntington's disease, or the worker had a BRCA1 gene that predisposed her to breast and ovarian cancer. People with family histories of certain diseases have had difficulty in buying health insurance.

【譯文】：基因測試已經有發展，然而，雇主與保險公司卻利用這點來處罰人們。已有幾個報導是有關於民眾無法獲得工作或被解僱，只因為他／她的父親或母親有杭廷頓舞蹈症，或是員工被診斷出帶有BRCA1基因，使她容易得到乳癌或是卵巢癌，而受到不平等待遇。帶有家族某些疾病歷史的民眾要買健康保險也不是那麼容易。

【解析】：（1）增譯：「而受到不平等待遇」。

（2）正說反譯：have had difficulty in buying health insurance 要買健康保險也不是那麼容易。

（3）Huntington's disease 杭廷頓病或杭廷頓舞蹈症

第三段：

【原文】：The Genetic Information Nondiscrimination Act ushers in a new era. The law prohibits employers from asking for genetic tests or taking into account an employee's genetic background in hiring, firing or promotions. It prohibits discrimination on the basis of genetic background in group and individual health insurance plans.

【譯文】：基因資訊反歧視法案開創了一個新世代。該法案禁止雇主要求雇員做基因測試，也禁止雇主在徵人、解僱、升遷時，將員工基因背景納入考量。有關群體或個人的健保計畫，此法案防止基於基因背景這方面的歧視。

【解析】：（1）重組：The law prohibits employers from asking for genetic tests or taking into account an employee's genetic background in hiring, firing or promotions. 該法案禁止雇主要求雇員做基因測試，也禁止雇主在徵人、解僱、升遷時，將員工基因背景納入考量。

（2）on the basis of 根據；以……為基礎；基於……

第四段：

【原文】：Some insurance companies and business groups opposed the law, arguing that it was unfair and unnecessarily burdensome.

But the Senate passed it unanimously, and the House with only one "no" vote, because lawmakers rightly saw that fairness and public policy arguments demanded a ban on discriminating against people for genetic traits they can do nothing about.

【譯文】：有一些保險公司和商業團體反對這項法案，他們認為這法案沒有公平性可言，而且根本沒有存在的必要，反而造成諸多困擾。然而參議院一致通過這項法案，眾議院也只有一個反對票，因為立法者公正地理解這項法案的公平性，而且諸多公共政策議題要求一個針對這類歧視的法令，來幫助帶有基因特徵卻無計可施的人。

【解析】：（1）改變詞性：it was unfair and unnecessarily burdensome 沒有公平性可言，而且根本沒有存在的必要，反而造成諸多困擾。

（2）重組：and public policy arguments demanded a ban on discriminating against people for genetic traits they can do nothing about 而且諸多公共政策議題要求一個針對這類歧視的法令，來幫助帶有基因特徵卻無計可施的人。

中譯英一般文件筆譯類（一）

【原文】：從去年9月的金融海嘯後，美國政府幾乎是用灑鈔票的方式來救經濟，美元匯價因此江河日下。如果紙幣再也無法成為個人財富的保證，那麼哪一種財富，不會像紙幣一樣在金融危機後蒸發，而且能保值，甚至在未來還可能增值呢？

答案就是「資源」，也就是「實物」，特別是那些珍貴又奇缺的資源。「資源」並不只侷限於人們熟知的石油、黃金等，事實上它涵蓋的概念相當廣泛，從燃料資源如石油、天然氣、煤炭；到森林資源如原木；礦物資源如鐵、鋁、銅等，以及貴金屬如金、銀、白金等，甚至足以生產大量農作物的土地，都是資源。

這些實實在在的資源蘊藏量有限，只會愈來愈值錢。實際上，那些持有鉅額美元外匯存底國家，包括中國、印度、日本等，早已體認到：未來，實物比鈔票更有力量；與其坐視手上財富隨美元貶值而不斷縮水，不如及早去投資實際的資源，因為擁有實物，才有未來影響全球的力量。

【譯文】：Since the financial crisis which occurred last September, the US government has been saving the economy by giving out a great deal of money. Therefore, the exchange rate of US dollar declined steadily. If the paper bill cannot become a guarantee of personal wealth anymore, then what kind of wealth will not be worthless like paper bills after financial crisis and will maintain its value, and even possibly increase its value in the future?

The answer is resources, also called material objects, especially the resources that are precious and incredibly rare. Resources are not only limited to those which people usually know about, such as oil and gold. In fact, the concept of resources is considerably broad: from fuel resources like petroleum, natural gas and coal, to forest resources like logs, mineral resources like iron, aluminum and copper, and precious metals like gold, silver and platinum, even including lands that can yield a large number of crops. All of these mentioned above can be regarded as resources.

These reserves of real resources are quite limited; they will only become valuable all the more. In fact, those countries that actually possess a large sum of money in foreign exchange reserves, including China, India and Japan, have already realized that material objects are more powerful than banknotes. People would rather invest on the real resources before it is too late than let their wealth continue shrinking with the depression of US dollar. It is because if people possess material objects, they will have power that may influence the whole world in the future.

第一段：

【原文】：從去年9月的金融海嘯後，美國政府幾乎是用灑鈔票的方式來救經濟，美元匯價因此江河日下。如果紙幣再也無法成為個人財富的保證，那麼哪一種財富，不會像紙幣一樣在金融危機後蒸發，而且能保值，甚至在未來還可能增值呢？

【譯文】：Since the financial crisis which occurred last September, the US government has been saving the economy by giving out a great deal of money. Therefore, the exchange rate of US dollar declined steadily. If the paper bill cannot become a guarantee of personal wealth anymore, then what kind of wealth will not be worthless like paper bills after financial crisis and will maintain its value, and even possibly increase its value in the future?

【解析】：（1）金融海嘯 financial tsunami, financial crisis, financial tidal wave

（2）轉譯：灑；分發；散發 to give out

（3）大量的／許多的錢 a great deal of money

（4）拆句：美元匯價因此江河日下。Therefore, the exchange rate of USD declined steadily.

（5）江河日下 to go from bad to worse, to be on the decline, to decline steadily

（6）紙幣 paper money, a paper bill, a paper currency, a note

（7）增值 to rise or increase in value, to appreciate

（8）財富 wealth, fortune, riches

第二段：

【原文】：答案就是「資源」，也就是「實物」，特別是那些珍貴又奇缺的資源。「資源」並不只侷限於人們熟知的石油、黃金等，事實上它涵蓋的概念相當廣泛，從燃料資源如石油、天然氣、煤炭；到森林資源如原木；礦物資源如鐵、鋁、銅等，以及貴金屬如金、銀、白金等，甚至足以生產大量農作物的土地，都是資源。

【譯文】：The answer is resources, also called material objects, especially the resources that are precious and incredibly rare. Resources are not only limited to those which people usually know about, such as oil and gold. In fact, the concept of resources is considerably broad: from fuel resources like petroleum, natural gas and coal, to forest resources like logs, mineral resources like iron, aluminum and copper, and precious metals like gold, silver and platinum, even including lands that can yield a large number of crops. All of these mentioned above can be regarded as resources.

【解析】：（1）實物 material objects

（2）拆句：「事實上它涵蓋的概念相當廣泛」譯為"In

fact, the concept of resources is considerably broad." 。

（3）大量的 a large number, a great quantity, a great deal (of), a world of, considerable quantities

第三段：

【原文】：這些實實在在的資源蘊藏量有限，只會愈來愈值錢。實際上，那些持有鉅額美元外匯存底國家，包括中國、印度、日本等，早已體認到：未來，實物比鈔票更有力量；與其坐視手上財富隨美元貶值而不斷縮水，不如及早去投資實際的資源，因為擁有實物，才有未來影響全球的力量。

【譯文】：These reserves of real resources are quite limited; they will only become valuable all the more. In fact, those countries that actually possess a large sum of money in foreign exchange reserves, including China, India and Japan, have already realized that material objects are more powerful than banknotes. People would rather invest on the real resources before it is too late than let their wealth continue shrinking with the depression of US dollar. It is because if people possess material objects, they will have power that may influence the whole world in the future.

【解析】：（1）蘊藏量 reserves

（2）外匯存底 foreign exchange reserves

中譯英一般文件筆譯類（二）

【原文】：髮線大撤退　保髮要趁早

髮型是上班族塑造外在形象的一大重點。但對有落髮問題、M字額日益明顯的男士來說，如何保住髮量恐怕才是當務之急。

皮膚科陳醫師就表示，門診中常見有落髮困擾的男性，因花了一、二十萬元做所謂的健髮課程無效，而前來就診。

陳醫師說，許多人常以爲中年以後才會有落髮的問題，但其實擔心自己髮線愈來愈後退而就醫的年輕人也不少。年輕患者若能在掉髮程度尚輕時及早接受治療，就能幫助維持原有髮量。但若錯過黃金時間，拖到已是「電火球」時才就醫，就算是想靠植髮來補救，往往也來不及了。

陳醫師指出，治療上首重調整生活形態；若長期壓力過大、抽菸，或飲食不均衡，都會讓頭髮掉得特別厲害。其次，也可在洗頭時以指腹輕輕按摩頭皮，促進血液循環。

若上述保健頭髮的方式仍無法有效減緩掉髮，可再加上生髮水或口服藥物治療。這兩種藥物都得自費，費用各約每月2,000元。雖不至於造成難以承受的經濟負擔，但因都必須持續使用才能維持生髮效果，一旦半途而廢，頭髮就會繼續掉落，所以需要耐心地長期抗戰。

【譯文】：**Hairlines are getting higher. It is better to prevent hair from losing as early as possible.**

Hairstyle is one key point to shape the external image of office workers. However, how to keep hair from losing is incredibly urgent to those men who have hair-losing problem and an increasingly obvious M word on their forheads.

Doctor Chen, a terminologist, said that it is often seen in clinic that men who have hair-losing problems come to see him because they spend about one hundred to two hundred thousand dollars taking what is called hair-caring courses but in vain.

Doctor Chen argued that many people often think that hair-losing problems appear after they step into the middle age. Nonetheless, quite a few young people, in fact, worry about their hairlines getting higher and go to see doctors. If young patients receive treatment as early as possible before the hair-losing problem gets serious, their original hair volume can be maintained. If they miss the optimum timing and do not go to see the doctor until "a lightening ball" is shown on their head, it can be too late for them to get their hair back even if they seek for the remedy of hair transplant.

Doctor Chen pointed out that, first of all, adjusting the lifestyle plays a major role in treatment. All of the bad habits, such as being under pressure for a long time, smoking and having unbalanced diet can make you lose your hair more seriously. Next, you can slightly massage your scalp with finger pulps in order to promote blood circulation.

If these hair-caring methods mentioned above cannot effectively slow down hair-losing problems, you can receive treatment by using tonic or taking medicine which cost you about 2,000 dollars a month respecctivley, which you need to pay for them yourself. Although it will not result in an unbearable economic burden, it is necessary to constantly use them in order to keep hair growing effect. If you give up halfway, your hair will continue losing. Therefore, it requires patience for you to prepare for the long fight.

第一段：

【原文】：**髮線大撤退　保髮要趁早**

髮型是上班族塑造外在形象的一大重點。但對有落髮問題、M字額日益明顯的男士來說，如何保住髮量恐怕才是當務之急。

【譯文】：**Hairlines are getting higher. It is better to prevent hair from losing as early as possible.**

Hairstyle is one key point to shape the external image of office workers. However, how to keep hair from losing is incredibly urgent to those men who have hair-losing problem and an increasingly obvious M word on their forheads.

第二段：

【原文】：皮膚科陳醫師就表示，門診中常見有落髮困擾的男性，因花了一、二十萬元做所謂的健髮課程無效，而前來就診。

【譯文】：Doctor Chen, a terminologist, said that it is often seen in clinic that men who have hair-losing problems come to see him because they spend about one hundred to two hundred thousand dollars taking what is called hair-caring courses but in vain.

第三段：

【原文】：陳醫師說，許多人常以為中年以後才會有落髮的問題，但其實擔心自己髮線愈來愈後退而就醫的年輕人也不少。年輕患者若能在掉髮程度尚輕時及早接受治療，就能幫助維持原有髮量。但若錯過黃金時間，拖到已是「電火球」時才就醫，就算是想靠植髮來補救，往往也來不及了。

【譯文】：Doctor Chen argued that many people often think that hair-losing problems appear after they step into the middle age. Nonetheless, quite a few young people, in fact, worry about their hairlines getting higher and go to see doctors. If young patients receive treatment as early as possible before the hair-losing problem gets serious, their original hair volume can be maintained. If they miss the optimum timing and do not go to see the doctor until "a lightening ball" is shown on their head, it can be too late for them to get their hair back even if they seek for the remedy of hair transplant.

【解析】：……以後才 not until

Many people often think that they do not have hair-losing problem until they step into the middle age.

第四段：

【原文】：陳醫師指出，治療上首重調整生活形態；若長期壓力過大、抽菸，或飲食不均衡，都會讓頭髮掉得特別厲害。其次，也可在洗頭時以指腹輕輕按摩頭皮，促進血液循環。

【譯文】：Doctor Chen pointed out that, first of all, adjusting the life-style plays a major role in treatment. All of the bad habits, such as being under pressure for a long time, smoking and having unbalanced diet can make you lose your hair more seriously. Next, you can slightly massage your scalp with finger pulps in order to promote blood circulation.

第五段：

【原文】：若上述保健頭髮的方式仍無法有效減緩掉髮，可再加上生髮水或口服藥物治療。這兩種藥物都得自費，費用各約每月2,000元。雖不至於造成難以承受的經濟負擔，但因都必須持續使用才能維持生髮效果，一旦半途而廢，頭髮就會繼續掉落，所以需要耐心地長期抗戰。

【譯文】：If these hair-caring methods mentioned above cannot effectively slow down hair-losing problems, you can receive treatment by using tonic or taking medicine which cost you about 2,000 dollars a month respecctivley, which you need to pay for them yourself. Although it will not result in an unbearable economic burden, it is necessary to constantly use them in order to keep hair growing effect. If you give up halfway, your hair will continue losing. Therefore, it requires patience for you to prepare for the long fight.

【解析】：半途而廢 to give up halfway, to drop/fall by the wayside, to stop half way

　　編者認為，翻譯作品的良窳取決於四個要素：第一是字彙量（vocabulary size），第二是翻譯方法與技巧（translation approaches and skills），第三是中英文造詣（Chinese and English competence），第四則是廣博閱讀與練習（extensive reading and practices）。而這四個要素環環相扣，互為因果。第一，增進字彙量的方法之一是熟悉字源學（etymology）或構詞學（morphology），若能掌握英文字源（即字首、字根、字尾）的邏輯性，可快速地記誦英文單字。第二，翻譯方法與技巧方面，請讀者參考本書中所提及的三個方法與六個技巧，綜合運用Adding Approach（增加法），Subtracting Approach（減少法），Transforming Approach（轉換法）或Changing Skill（改變技巧），Splitting Skill（拆句技巧），Combining Skill（合併技巧），Affirmative/Negative Switching Skill（肯定句否定句交換技巧），Restructuring Skill（重組技巧），Synthesizing Skill（綜合技巧）。第三，中英文造詣的提升，與大量閱讀與練習相關。最後一個要素，在廣博閱讀方面，讀者可以選擇較輕鬆的讀物，因為學理與中外實證研究結果均顯示，「悅讀」（rcading for pleasure, reading for fun）的效果最好。

Steve Jobs口頭報告成功的其中一個祕訣就是 "Re-hearse, rehearse, and rehearse." 他每次上臺前一定會練習、練習再練習。翻譯是需要學習與練習的，許多專家學者都持相同的看法。編者殷切希望以上的教學經驗與心得，能有助於提升學生的中英文翻譯品質與效率。學生若能藉由廣博翻譯（extensive translation）、密集翻譯（intensive translation）、專業翻譯（specific translation）循序漸進，配合學習與練習上述的翻譯方法與技巧，假以時日，就可以熟能生巧，提升翻譯與口譯的能力。

Alec Ross曾是Hilary Clinton的資深顧問，他在2016年的新書*The Future of Industries*（《未來產業》）中提到以下三種能力非常重要：（1）Critical and Analytical Skills（批判與分析能力）；（2）Language Skill（programming language and foreign languages）（程式設計語言與外語能力）；（3）Life-long learning（終身學習的能力）。期盼本書能協助讀者提升以上所提到的三種能力，進而成為具有高競爭力的現代知識經濟人。

參考文獻

1. 梅德明（2010）。*Interpreting for general purposes*。北京：北京大學出版社。

2. 吳潛誠（1989）。中英翻譯：對比分析法。臺北：文鶴出版有限公司。

3. 思果（2003）。翻譯研究。臺北：大地出版社。

4. 思果（2013）。翻譯新究（第六版）。臺北：大地出版社。

5. 林語堂（1967）。論翻譯。無所不談合集。臺北：天地圖書。

6. 王斌華、伍志偉（2014）。漢英口譯：轉換技能進階。北京：外語教學與研究出版社。

7. 李智燕（2006）。*iBT*托福應考聖經：閱讀測驗。（*Longman iBT TOEFL: Reading*）。臺北：培生出版公司。

8. Aberhart, G. (2014). Where the ocean meets the mountains – Qingshui Cliff. *Taiwan Panorama, 39* (8), pp. 80-85.

9. About Chinese Language. (2017). Autumn Thoughts: To the Tune of Tian Jin Sha. Retrieved September 15, 2017, from http://www.xcn-chinese.com/app/showarticle.asp?id=691&includeid=&siteid=.

10. BBC News. (2016). *Yemen in crisis: Who is fighting whom?* Retrieved July 17, 2016, from http://www.bbc.com/news/world-middle-east-29319423.

11. Catford, J. C. (1965). *A linguistic theory of translation*. London: Oxford University Press.

12. CNA. (2015). *Chinese coast guard vessels patrol Diaoyutai waters*. Retrieved July 17, 2016, from http://focustaiwan.tw/search/201508020018.aspx?q=bear.

13. Editorial Board. (2015). *Greece's future and the Euro's*. The New York Times. Retrieved July 17, 2016, from http://www.nytimes.com/2015/06/30/opinion/greeces-future-and-the-euros.html?_r=0.

14. Halliday, M. A. K. & Hassan, R. (1976). *Cohesion in English*. London:

Longman.

15. Hope, K. (2015). *Facebook now used by half of world's online users*. BBC News. Retrieved July 17, 2016, from http://www.bbc.com/news/business-33712729.

16. Kaplan, R. (1966). Cultural thought patterns in intercultural education. *Language Learning, 16*, pp.1-20.

17. Moss. T. (2015). *Obama's missed Africa opportunity*. CNN. Retrieved July 17, 2016, from http://edition.cnn.com/2015/07/22/opinions/moss-obama-africa-visit/.

18. Nida, E. A. (1984). *Translating meaning*. San Dimas, California: English Language Institute.

19. Pakistan Defence. (2015). *KMT lawmakers threaten reprisal over Lee's Diayoutai comment*. Retrieved July 17, 2016, from http://defence.pk/threads/diaoyutai-islands-belong-to-taiwan-dpp-chairwoman.388710/.

20. Pease, B., & Pease A. (2006). *The definitive book of body language: The hidden meaning behind people's gestures and expressions*. NY: Bantam Dell.

21. Ross, A. (2016). *The industries of the future*. California: Simon & Schuster.

22. Shandong Transvoice Translation Co., Ltd. 「枯藤老樹昏鴉」翻譯爲何添加詞語？譯文3. 丁祖馨、Burtton Raffel 合譯. (2017). Retrieved September 15, 2017, from http://www.rzfanyi.com/ArticleShow.asp?ArtID=955。

23. Smith, D., & Williams, S. (2014). Remaking our world – Outstanding Taiwanese women in science. *Taiwan Panorama, 39* (8), pp. 66-70.

24. Stamouli, N., Bouras, S., & Steinhauser, G. (2015). *Greece's Parliament Passes Austerity Measures Required for Bailout*. The Wall Street Journal. Retrieved July 17, 2016, from http://www.wsj.com/articles/

greeces-parliament-passes-austerity-measures-required-for-bail-out-1437002734.

25. Taipei Times. (2015). *Smartphone detox.* Retrieved July 17, 2016, from http://www.taipeitimes.com/News/lang/print/2015/06/20/2003621091.

26. Taipei Times. (2015). *Pay your fine and get a helmet.* Retrieved July 17, 2016, from http://www.taipeitimes.com/News/lang/archives/2015/06/17/2003620855.

27. Taipei Times. (2015). *Yilan's eco park.* Retrieved July 17, 2016, from http://www.taipeitimes.com/News/lang/archives/2015/06/16/2003620778.

28. Taipei Times. (2015). *What is the best thing for your back? Standing.* Retrieved July 17, 2016, http://www.taipeitimes.com/News/lang/archives/2015/06/13/2003620546.

29. Taipei Times. (2015). *Typing style reveals fatigue.* Retrieved July 17, 2016, from http://www.taipeitimes.com/News/lang/archives/2015/05/20/2003618670.

30. Taipei Times. (2015). *Film crew's shooting scares rare crane.* Retrieved July 17, 2016, from http://www.taipeitimes.com/News/lang/archives/2015/05/19/2003618591.

31. Tan, C-L. (2001). Language teaching and translation. In S-W Chan & D. E. Pollard (Eds.), *An encyclopedia of translation* (pp. 476-486). Hong Kong: The Chinese University Press.

32. The Guardian. (2015). *Iran nuclear deal: world powers reach historic agreement to lift sanctions.* Retrieved July 17, 2016, from https://www.theguardian.com/world/2015/jul/14/iran-nuclear-programme-world-powers-historic-deal-lift-sanctions.

33. Webb, J. (2015). *'Leaders and lifters' help ants move massive meals.* BBC News. Retrieved July 17, 2016, from http://www.bbc.com/news/33692054.

参考文獻

34. Wikipedia. (2016). *Translation*. Retrieved July 17, 2016, from https://en.wikipedia.org/wiki/Translation.

實用中英翻譯法

筆記頁

國家圖書館出版品預行編目資料

實用中英翻譯法／彭登龍著. －－初版. －－
臺北市：五南，2017.12
　面；　公分
ISBN 978-957-11-9529-2（平裝）

1.英語　2.翻譯

805.1　　　　　　　　　　106024251

1X5G

實用中英翻譯法

作　　　者— 彭登龍（277.5）

發 行 人— 楊榮川

總 經 理— 楊士清

副總編輯— 黃文瓊

主　　編— 朱曉蘋

編　　輯— 吳雨潔

封面設計— 謝瑩君

出 版 者— 五南圖書出版股份有限公司

地　　址：106台北市大安區和平東路二段339號4樓

電　　話：(02)2705-5066　　傳　　真：(02)2706-6100

網　　址：http://www.wunan.com.tw

電子郵件：wunan@wunan.com.tw

劃撥帳號：01068953

戶　　名：五南圖書出版股份有限公司

法律顧問　林勝安律師事務所　林勝安律師

出版日期　2017年12月初版一刷

定　　價　新臺幣320元